Dreadmyre

Emberwall, Book 1

J.A. Raikes

ISBN-13: 978-1-7341476-0-5

V,

Thanks for always believing in me, even if hiking isn't really my thing.

CHAPTER ONE

Ever wonder what it takes to be in a book? To have your life jotted down by someone because you did something worth remembering? I wouldn't say that it's something I ever wanted or dreamed of. Truth be told, I wasn't really looking for anything spectacular to happen. I only wrote this down to help me process what the heck happened to me. That doesn't change the fact that a lot has happened and the only logical place I can think to start this little adventure I call my life is back in the good old days.

My name is Finnegan Benjamin Riley, though I typically go by Finn. Not a flashy name, but certainly not standard by any stretch. Since I'm not sitting there in front of you sharing this little tale, you'd probably like to know a little about me. I'm not one for spending much time talking about myself, so bear with me while I fumble my way through this.

I'm a relatively average guy. Others describe me as "lanky" - which is a kind way of saying I look unnaturally thin for how tall I am, considering I'm only 130 pounds and none of it is fat or muscle. I started working out recently, though, but the results are slow going. My sandy brown hair doesn't stay put no matter how hard I try to style it. I'd like to think it makes me ruggedly handsome, but most ladies argue that it makes me look "greasy." Anyway, I don't feel like I have much else to say that won't make its way out in the pages of this book. My personality just *shines* on paper. Okay, not really, but like I said, I'm not actually that into sharing about me.

Here's my guess at a bit about you, because you're not sitting in front of me for me to read your expressions and know when to shut my big mouth and change tone so I don't bore you to death: you like to read (really went out on a limb for that one, huh?). Something about reading takes you away from the mundane chores that keep you down during the day - maybe it's school and you're just not interested in "the quadratic formula" and the various applications your teacher swears it has for "the real world." Perhaps you're working and just want to unwind at the end of the day and a good story is your way of leaving the stress of the day behind. Or maybe you're an adrenaline junkie and interested in a story which leaves your breath hanging somewhere between your lungs and the gaping maw of your open mouth. Well here's my deal for you, you avid reader, you. You hang on for the ride and I won't judge you for leaving your hot beverage on the table so long it cooled off and is totally gross now. I'm kidding, (I will judge you) but in any event here we go - here's a shot at explaining what you're in for...

It was the year...well, it doesn't really matter what it was, does it? The world was much the same as it had always been. New talking heads trying to control the masses with each side trying to one-up the other. Power changed hands a bunch of times while I was a kid, but the world itself changed very little. I grew up in Tucson, Arizona - for which the best thing that can be said is that it is not Phoenix since that place might as well be the surface of the sun for anyone unfortunate enough to step outside during the summer.

Tucson is one of those odd places. It has a strange and charming allure to it. One part retirement community over the top of something ancient and mysterious. From ages past, Tucson was home to the Tohono O'odham, a revered and powerful group of Native Americans. Most of the land Tucson now occupies was once their sacred ground and if you look long enough, you find the handiwork of these people dotting the landscape - small hovels once housing a family now permanently etched on the horizon, or the beautiful designs of their culture inserted into the modern desert vogue. The impact is subtle, but if you ever choose to leave, the desert draws you back like an invisible undercurrent whose presence is only noticed once it has swept you up into its power. Everyone I knew growing up who left, young or old, always ended up coming back to their roots in Tucson. I was one of the few from my high school that even attempted to leave Tucson but I, too, was drawn back. When I returned, I found few others had left.

Ever since I returned, I've grown to love Tucson. I'm a bit of an outdoor junkie and Tucson has no shortage of places to explore outside. As a matter of fact, Tucson isn't what most people expect when they travel to a "desert." Sure, it qualifies as a desert by the technical definition (which, for those of you who live pretty much anywhere else here's a fun fact to lock in your noggin - to classify as a "desert," there must be less than 10 inches of rain a year on average. The more ya know.) Truth be told, Tucson has way more going for it than rolling dunes and sand everywhere.

Allow me to paint you a picture: The town is smack in the center of a valley, surrounded on all sides by mountains. The people brave enough to try and settle in the desert figured out that the ancient tribes who first dwelled there were onto something with their home design. As such, adobe brick buildings pay homage to the Natives, while a mix of contemporary homes and businesses show a desire to stick with the times. As the town spreads out, small communities grow next to one another, giving a unique personality to every neighborhood, and every few blocks, there are intentional art pieces designed to draw you back to the beauty of the desert landscape. To a point, most of the buildings around town are painted with neutral earth tones to avoid distracting from the view of nature that wraps completely around the city with mountains.

To the south, the Santa Rita mountain range pokes its head on the horizon - it is by far the furthest from the city and if you want to get there, you're not likely to still be in Tucson, proper. Rumor has it, most of the "shady business" that occurs in the area tends to go down near those peaks. But still, they're something to look at.

To the far east, the Rincon mountain range wraps around the city with rolling hills and occasional peaks which dot the horizon. As if two mountain ranges weren't enough, directly next to the city itself is the Santa Catalina mountain range. If you've ever been to Tucson, you know the sight. Sharp peaks and deep crags litter the landscape. Dotted with brush, buffelgrass (a sort of bushy, dead looking fern), mesquite trees and loads of limestone, the Catalina mountains stretch upwards of nine thousand feet at some of its summits. The mountains have become hotspots for tourists and natives alike for any number of adventurous pastimes. If you're the outdoorsy type like me, all you need to do is point to a peak or destination and go for it. Chances are good someone else has paved the way and you can follow a rough (or well-traveled) path to your heart's delight. In any event, I digress. You get the idea, so I'll spare you the details of all the other mountains that surround my hometown, because there are plenty more to talk about and I'm known to be a bit long winded.

The native wildlife is just as varied - mountain lions blend in with the natural tones of the cliff side to stalk their prey and birds have adapted by cracking open some of the hardest seeds on Earth for a bite to eat before carving out a home in the middle of a spined Saguaro cactus. There are deer and lizards, hawks and squirrels, pack rats and coyote coexisting and surviving under the harsh sun. There is even a boar-like creature called a javelina (pronounced have-uh-lee-nah). It's basically an overgrown bristleback brown pig with tusks that has a rank stench you can smell for hours after it has passed by. The things are nearly blind and incredibly stupid, but if you aren't paying attention, it's possible to be mauled by one on an early morning walk around the neighborhood. Thankfully, they typically keep to themselves.

Of all the treasures that Tucson has to offer, none is more precious or beautiful than the sunset. I was told as a kid it had something to do with the right settings atmospherically and the dryness of the environment (*"it's a dry heat!"*) that enables the sunsets to look the way they do. I don't remember all the science stuff and frankly, I don't care. The reality is, you'll never experience a sunset in the entire world as you will in Tucson. The sky ripples with anticipation as the sun slowly dips beneath the horizon, finally letting the ground below cool down from a day of heat and strife. But those few moments when the sun and the sky are in harmony - man, you cannot find a painter who can do it justice or a photo which can capture it's enormity. The late afternoon nearly explodes with an array of colors that vividly shift every moment with such clarity that the entire city is compelled by mother nature herself to stop moving for just a moment to appreciate her beauty. Truly, there is nothing on earth as magical as a Tucson sunset.

Or at least, that's what I thought.

It's funny how easy it is to go on and on about home when you miss it. When I was young, I was always told that horrible cliche "you never know what you're missing until it's gone!" I think as kids, we have a tendency to ignore these things because we don't have to miss life - we are living it. But with age comes perspective and an appreciation for the bygones. And my parents, teachers, and mentors were all right - you really have no idea what you're missing until it's gone.

I once spent a few years in living in Chicago and fell in love with the big city. The skyscrapers, the hustle and bustle and all the people knowing where they were going and looking sharp while they were doing it. I never wanted to leave. But every now and then, when someone asked me where I was from, I couldn't help but be drawn to the idea of a Tucson sunset. I knew that I'd eventually be back there. It was home.

So I went back. I left the Windy City and headed to the Old Pueblo. I moved back in with my parents and lived the dream, working a 9-to-5 job with zero prospects of any kind of advancement or a fulfilling career in sight. I was living in a small portion of my parent's house, sectioned off by a curtain rod and a single drape in order to give me some sort of "privacy." I'd leave every morning and head to my cubicle at the office. I'd plop down at my desk and stare at a mountain of invoices to process and phone calls to make. The little red light on the work phone flicked on and off, reminding me I had about six-trillion messages to listen to with customers yelling at my answering machine. Yep, living as a 20 something with my parents, and seeing no hope for change in the future. "Don't worry kids, life gets better!" Or so they say.

Once you climb out of the mound of crippling student debt, perhaps you can finally start looking for a job that doesn't seem to take away your soul with every ring of the telephone.

"Hi, this is Finn, how can I help you today?"

Or perhaps...

"Hi, Mr. I-dont-know-or-care I heard you were unsatisfied with your last visit from our technician. Let me assure you that it is always our goal to make sure you are highly satisfied with your experience and I'm calling to see how we can make sure you're highly satisfied. Oh? You want your next month of service free and a bunch of other free things in order to fix some perceived wrong you encountered when we showed up? Perfect, that'll just come out of my wages and we'll be all set."

Or maybe even better...

"Of course we will come back out immediately to make sure that things are done exactly the way you, the untrained non-technician, would like it to be done, even though that is against federal regulations we are ethically bound to. No no, please, allow us to take the fall for that one."

Yeah, okay, so perhaps I have a few bitter

feelings towards that job.

Still, it was a chance to be home and I was actually enjoying living with my parents. It's not ideal for most people my age, but it saved money and my parents are probably the nicest people you've met. My mom is the kind of woman who will invite you over for dinner and insist that you get what you want. She's making pasta but you're feeling like a steak? Great, she'll make the pasta and grab you a steak and throw it on the grill. Need veggies with that? She'll find what's freshest and cook it up for you. See something in the cupboard you like? It's yours and please, if there isn't enough for you, let her know because she'll go out and get you more. My mom is just that kind of a lady.

My dad, on the other hand, is a gentle man. He will listen to you for hours and ask questions to find out about you while mentally creating a whole slew of chores for himself to get done in order to make your life easier. Because undoubtedly, in your stories, you've poured out your heart to him and he knows that you need your plumbing fixed or your vents checked or your computer reprogrammed or a new desk built from this random log you found at a discount thrift store.

He'll get it all done for you today and won't complain a lick. Oh, and have I mentioned he's completely blind? No big deal - he only deconstructs computer programs for a living doing cybersecurity without seeing it.

Okay okay, I'll stop - you get the picture. They're wonderful people and I loved spending time with them.

The thing is, though, that everything else about my family is somewhat shrouded in mystery. My parents told me stories of their families when I was young, but by the time I was ten, the entirety of my extended family were no longer in the picture. My grandfather on my dad's side went missing when my father was young, right around the time he lost his sight. The police marked it as a cold case after a few months and slowly resources dedicated to the case were cut and ultimately stopped altogether. According to dad, his mom was never the same afterward. She stayed strong for him as much as she was able, helping him with school work and trying to make life as easy as possible for a young man with a newfound disability. But slowly over time, she slipped away - mentally at first, but her body followed soon after. She died at age 51. He was only 24.

My mom's family died young as well, though I did get the chance to meet them. We had spent several holidays with her family and it was always a fun time for me. When I was only five, however, my grandmother passed away around Thanksgiving and her husband a short while later. I remember going to their funerals and told how wonderful their lives had been, though I barely knew them. So that left just me, my parents and our cat, Bruce.

Oh, have I not mentioned Bruce yet? He is awesome. Best cat you'd ever meet. A brown and speckled little dude, he is 8 pounds of fluff and joy. He loves everyone and cannot seem to get enough affection. I have had many nights with that giant fluff ball conked out on my lap while I'm doing...well, really, whatever. He can sleep through anything.

As for me, I was stuck in a dead end job and chances were good nothing was going to change for a while. So why am I putting this all in a book then? *Because you never know what you have until it's gone.*

CHAPTER TWO

Can I give you a tip? Don't choose the middle of summer to hike in the mountains of Tucson with only a gallon of water. Without question, it's one of the worst mistakes I've ever made.

I was on vacation from work. I needed a break from the monotony of answering phones and listening to everyone's problems while never able to help. Oh, the joys of customer service. I'm not sure who came up with the "The Customer is Always Right," but I had reached a place in my job where I felt strongly about finding that person and punching him in the throat.

Okay, so perhaps that is a bit extreme, but you get the picture.

I had worked a little over a year without a break and was ready to do some exploring. Growing up, I went camping with friends and their families and had really come to enjoy the solitude of the outdoors.

So I cobbled together a few things I would need for the journey. I owned a hiking pack, which is just a fancy backpack with extra pockets and specially designed to help make a day hike more like a walk in the park. It came with a medium-sized water pouch with a tube attached that could be threaded through the backpack so I had easy access to water without having to unpack the entire thing.

I filled the water pouch and tossed in a small blanket, an extra pair of shorts and loaded up on "trail rations" (that's my way of justifying taking a whole box of breakfast bars and a few handfuls of nuts, a bag of beef jerky and a half dozen or so fruit snacks).

I learned early on in my hiking career that wearing layers is an absolute must. There is no telling how the weather might change or what you might get caught in if a storm were to roll in quickly or the heat spiked unexpectedly. So I wore a light tank top and threw on a shirt made of that fancy breathable athletic material. It was summertime which in Tucson means triple-digit temps and nonstop sunshine, so I wasn't particularly concerned with a sudden burst of rain.

Having loaded up, I left a note on my desk so my parents would have an idea that I was going to be gone for a day or two on this hike. I hopped in my car and headed to the nearest trailhead.

It was only a few miles to the entrance of the Catalina State Park public area. I drove to the entrance and paid my dues to the attendant at the booth guarding the forest against freeloaders. I've never been entirely sure how those guys were going to stop anything from happening in several thousand acres of the park from their booth, but hey, I suppose it deters someone? In any event, I headed down the road until I came to the designated parking area.

If you haven't been on a hike in a state park, let me draw you into the glory of state-protected mother nature: There are gorgeous views as far as the eye can see (as long as you don't look back to where you drove in from) and relatively untouched nature everywhere. In the Catalinas, this means cacti blooming with orange and pink flowers, small plants covered in yellow-greens and browns and there is wildlife *everywhere*. As you enter, a few dirt trails branch off in several directions, depending on the type of hike you're interested in and the level of intensity you'd prefer. I've been hiking most of my life and while I'm not especially in-shape from sitting at a desk every day answering phones, I have made it a priority to get to the gym a few times a week. So I chose a trail that I've taken a few times, knowing in about three miles I'd have a couple of options as to how far into the park I would like to go. I was looking for overnight camping, so I knew the general direction I would need to go to get away from the crowds of weekend-warriors trying their hand at being outdoorsy.

I set a good pace for a while, covering quite a bit of ground in a short amount of time. Being "lanky" helps when you want to get a move on quickly. The sun beat down on me and in no time, I worked up a healthy sweat. I kept up the pace for a while until the trail thinned and there was only the occasional other hiker that would pass by. Typically, I don't like to rush through a hike. I feel like it defeats the purpose of enjoying nature if you're just in it for the destination, but at the same time, I also like to make a quick break from the pack.

In about half an hour, I reached a trail marker placed by the rangers, detailing info about the different destinations ahead. The sign read, "Romero pools, 2.8 miles. Romero Pass 6.4 miles. Split Mt. Lemmon trail & West Fork Sabino Trail." The most popular trail on this branch of the park was for the pools and I knew from experience that most hikers would stop there for a rest and then turn back to head home. It was about a two-hour hike just to the pools, and I decided I would head towards the Mt. Lemmon trail, which would take a few more hours beyond that. It was hot out and there would be more options for shade once I got past the pools.

As I trekked onward, I took occasional breaks for rest and refueling, breaking into the box of breakfast bars and taking occasional sips from my water. Most people surprisingly don't realize that dehydration is your biggest enemy when you're hiking in Arizona. There are a ton of poisonous creatures and scary predators like diamondback rattlesnakes and mountain lions but you're less likely to be harmed by anything like that if you're paying attention to where you're going. Instead, it's the dehydration that ends up catching more people off guard because they don't think to drink water until they're thirsty. Take a tip from a Tucson native - if you're thirsty, you're already dehydrated and you're fighting an uphill battle to replenish those fluids. The key to successful hiking in a hot climate is to drink even when you're not thirsty so your body doesn't start shutting down before you think to refuel it.

I continued onward for a few miles, enjoying the desert landscape and the occasional bird or small critter I came across. I passed Romero Pools and stopped to enjoy the strangest of sights you can see in Tucson: standing water. The pools aren't large and by the summertime, they're usually mostly dried up, but the mountains do get a light dusting of snow in the winter and the runoff is the chief source of water for these pools. A few young couples and a family with several kids were enjoying the pools today. The kids were splashing and playing in the water and the adults were eating a picnic lunch. I took a few minutes to enjoy the sights and rest under a palo verde tree and then I was up and going again, continuing through to Romero Pass for an hour or so.

Everything seemed to be going well. I was alone in nature and I could literally feel the tension in my shoulders and back seeping out of my muscles from sitting in that horrible desk chair. I could breathe easy, knowing there were no angry customers for miles. The only thing I had to think about was where I wanted to go next, and I couldn't have been happier. I spent the bulk of the day meandering through the foothills of the mountain, enjoying the sights and being struck with whatever took my imagination.

Let me tell you, there are some simply incredibly beautiful flowers in the foothills of the Catalinas. Small purple lupines send shocks of color across the landscape, occasionally poking their heads out of bramble and thorns. California poppies force their way through the rocks with bright orange petals and palo verde trees spawn hundreds of beautiful (although allergy inducing) yellow buds that look like they're rippling up the mountainside. Then there's the cactus. Cacti, for all the spikes and thorns, can produce the most magnificent flowers with all sorts of colors and shapes. I often found myself blazing a trail through brush just to explore these beautiful sights. As I said, I think it's a waste to simply rush through a hike - you miss all the joys and beauty of nature. After all, that's why I left in the first place. I just needed something beautiful to take my mind off the worries of work.

The day was slowly fading into late afternoon and I decided that I should start looking for where I was going to stop for the night. I was miles from any recognizable civilization and it had been a good six hours since I'd last seen anyone else picking their way through the trail, so I decided to branch off the main path. There were dozens of choices for places to stop - a clearing here, an oddly grown mess of brush over there. I wanted to find somewhere secluded so I could rest without the chance of a stray trailblazer (like myself) stumbling over me.

As I delved deeper into the wilderness looking for the perfect place to set up camp, I grabbed the tube at my shoulder, coming from the water canister in my backpack and popped it in my mouth. I as I sucked on the straw, bursts of air sputtered in the tube. I shifted the pack on my back and gave the tube another try. More air pockets pulled through.

Great Finn. Really great.

My heart sank as I realized I had made a grievous error. I had packed food and a light blanket and made my way out into the middle of nowhere several hours away from anyone or anything. What dawned on me now was that I had failed to pack was extra water for the hike back.

It's okay, I reasoned with myself. *I'll just conserve what I have left and I'll leave in the early morning when it's coolest so I can get out before the heat of the day.* Logic, Finn. Sure, people have died out here because they didn't bring enough water. Sure, you've always made fun of them to yourself because you would never be so foolish as to be that unprepared. But you've been hiking for years! You'll be just fine. Your body is used to this and who knows, maybe you'll find some usable water out here.

Daylight was dwindling and the sky was lit up with the colorful array of purples, pinks and oranges of those classic Tucson sunsets. Lost in my thoughts trying to piece together a plan of action for the morning, I didn't take notice of the small ravine I was headed straight toward. The ground beneath me sloped dramatically and was covered in loose bits of shale rock. My foot hit a piece of the loose stone and went sailing out from under me and I slipped down the ravine. My heart lurched in my chest as I floundered and my body teetered for a few moments as I began practically rock surfing down the hill. Thankfully I was able to regain my balance before I fell and broke something, like an arm or my brain. I froze with my arms out at my sides for balance and let my heartbeat come back from mimicking the Kentucky Derby.

Good going, Finn. Now you're at the bottom of a cliff.

That'll teach me to be distracted. I quickly scanned the edge I'd just slid down for anything I could use to scramble back up. Given my current streak of personal victories, it came as no surprise that there didn't seem to be anything at the ready.

It doesn't look like you're getting up there any time soon, either. Thanks, brain.

I've learned over the years that one of the worst things you can do when something unexpected happens during a hike, or any kind of outdoor adventure for that matter, is to panic. So I steadied my balance, made sure I found purchase on a solid bit of ground and stopped to focus. My heart was beating in my ears and sweat trickled down the side of my face. Even though the sun was setting, heat still emanated from the ground and my body reacted in kind.

Breathing in my nose and out of my mouth, I worked to hone in on my surroundings.

Apparently, I slid down into a small gulch surrounded on all sides by sheer rock walls, save for the small area I had slid down. There was little chance that I was going to be able to climb back out any direction except the way I had entered. The issue with that, though, was the way out was completely covered with loose rock and would be incredibly challenging to clamber up in the darkness of the early morning if I was hoping to leave before the sun was up.

It was just at this moment that the reality of my *entire* situation dawned on me. Either I try to climb out of this pit in the dark and risk injuring myself, leaving me unable to hike out at all, or wait until it's light outside and risk dehydration, heat exhaustion and an unfortunate end to my vacation. To top it all off, as a way to try to calm down, I took another quick pull from my water tube holstered on the side of my backpack and was greeted with the wheezing sound of air bursting in between tiny sips of water, letting me know I was basically out of water at this point.

Great.

Remember how I mentioned that panicking is one of the worst ideas in this situation? A calm, level-headed focus is what gets you out of a tough situation. Well, it is a lot easier said than done. My pulse took off as I realized I was in very real danger. You might be lucky enough to survive out in the desert for a few days without food if you're well nourished first. Lacking water is a different situation entirely. The moment you run out of water, a countdown begins and you need to make a change quickly or you won't make it out at all.

I tried breathing to slow my pulse but reality comes for us all at some point. I looked around in the fading twilight to find something, anything, that might help me. Through the haze of my increasingly frantic state, I spotted a small opening in the side of the rock face in the back edge of the ravine. Something near the opening caught my eye, but I couldn't make it out in the fading light.

The ground at the bottom of the ravine was flat and sandy - probably the location of a small pool which had dried up in the summer heat. I had likely followed the path that the water would take and found myself at a similar dead end. I jogged toward the small opening in the rock and pulled up short when I noticed a piece of metal sticking out of the ground near the hole. I bent down and tried to pull it out of the sand, but met with too much resistance to actually move it. The metal must've been bigger than I thought or it was buried under a lot of sand. Either way, it was stuck and I wasn't going to make it budge. I'm not sure what I had hoped to accomplish, but I was pretty much going off of impulse at this point. I gave up on the metal and peered into the small opening in the rock. It was completely black inside and the fading sunlight wasn't helping.

I unslung one shoulder strap of my backpack, shifted the pack around to my chest and unzipped the front pouch. I dug through leftover wrappers from a previous hike, a few napkins and tissues and finally, my hand hit what I was looking for: my small LED flashlight. I pulled it out, depressed the button on the top and was met with a nearly imperceptibly dim glow from the bulbs. Thank goodness it still worked, if barely.

I dropped to my hands and knees and shined the light into the hole. I didn't really care what was in there, as long as it wasn't a hungry animal. Most creatures in the desert start to come out at night when it's cool so they can hunt and I didn't want to be a tasty treat for whatever took up residence at the bottom of this ravine. One problem at a time, right?

I couldn't make out much of what was in the

hole, but there didn't seem to be anything starting back at me, so I figured I was relatively safe. I only got a brief moment to check because the flashlight petered out almost as soon as I finished glancing around. I stood up and dusted off my pants and turned off the dead flashlight, simply out of habit. The best I could hope for at this point was to get a little rest and get out of this ravine without breaking my ankle and dying.

I zipped up my bag and tried to find a comfortable spot near the ravine wall to set up camp for the night. I scanned the ground around me for any more metal chunks poking out of the sand to make sure I didn't need a tetanus shot in addition to an IV of fluids. As I looked, caught a glint of something reflecting the light of the fading sun up off to my right. I turned to see, and that's when I saw the menacing reflective eyes of a mountain lion staring me down from the ledge above.

CHAPTER THREE

I wish that I could say I stayed calm, having been a "seasoned hiker" and spent a good deal of time in the outdoors. But I didn't. No, instead, I freaked out like a groupie at a rock concert. To be fair, I was already on edge because of my own stupidity. I wasn't exactly primed for success when being stared down by a mountain lion with its teeth bared. So I let out a quick scream and scrambled for options.

I don't know what compelled me to do what I did next - Bravery? Luck? Stupidity? A primal instinct which drives us humans to avoid being eaten alive by hungry wild animals?

Likely, it was a combination of all of the above. Well, except maybe bravery.

A second after I noticed the beast, the mountain lion bounded down the steep walls of the ravine directly toward me. I wasted no time. I sloughed off my backpack, dropped to my belly and wiggled my way through the small opening in the rock wall. I was really hoping that I hadn't missed something when I looked earlier, otherwise this was going to be a very short-lived plan of escape.

Once inside, I was surprised to find it was a lot bigger than I had originally thought. I couldn't really see much of anything, but I didn't care. I turned around, squatted and grabbed one of the straps of my backpack that was closest to the opening and yanked. As I did, the mountain lion couldn't have been more than a yard away. The backpack was bulky and awkward with the box of breakfast bars and all the other things I had stuffed in it. It got stuck in the opening of the hole and I tried yanking again and again to free it.

Turns out, this was a blessing in disguise. If I couldn't yank my pack into the cave, that meant the cat couldn't get me in here either. I wasn't going to bank on my pathetic canvas bag protecting me for very long and, while the lion outside was probably a good three or four times larger in bulk than me, I would guess that if it really wanted to get me for an evening snack, it would try to wiggle its way in here too. I pulled on the backpack one more time and managed to wedge it into the hold more tightly.

By sheer luck, though, I thankfully still had the flashlight clenched in my white-knuckled fist. Hoping beyond hope, I clicked the top button.

Nothing.

You'd think I would've remembered to check my flashlight batteries and, oh I don't know, pack enough water for an overnight hike? Forget that I ever mentioned that I was a smart and savvy hiker. I'm certain that at this point, I lost any boy scout badges I might have earned. I'd blame it on the crappy desk job messing with my sense of adventure, but it's more likely just my stupidity and not thinking ahead. I've been known to act or speak before thinking for most of my life. Perhaps I should reevaluate some of my life choices once I'm out of this mess...

I smacked the back of the flashlight against the palm of my hand several times and jiggled the edge of the bulb to make the connectors line up. I clicked the button again and this time, that dim white light pierced the dark cave once again. Thank god for Alkaline predictability. I knew that I probably only had moments before the light died again so as soon as it clicked on, I was on alert to figure out what I could use to hopefully make it out of here in one piece.

First things first, I found a stone resting near the hole I had crawled through. I grabbed at it and with a forceful heave, moved it just next to the entrance. I knew I needed to time the next part just right or I was going to be a kitty snack. I reached down, yanked hard on the strap of my backpack and using the momentum, rocked to one side and forced the rock through the sand in front of the opening so it blocked the entrance.

With relative safety secured for the moment, it was time to figure out the next steps. A glance around the small cavern revealed that it was not small at all. As a matter of fact, it was downright *huge*.

The walls of the cave were smooth stone. The sand under my feet near the opening transitioned a yard or so from where I stood to a smooth rock, as though someone had carved a room into the middle of this mountainside. It was a deep cavern which seemed to delve far into the mountain. More astounding than the surprising room-like nature of this cave was what was in the cave. In the center of the otherwise empty cavern stood a roughly one-story tall circular metal ring, overlaid with gemstones of various colors, resting on a solid metal base.

Um...what?

As I panned my flashlight over the contraption, the LED light faded, flickered and died once more. Of course.

I sighed with frustration and tried again in vain to get the flashlight to work. I clicked the button on the top again and again and smacked the flashlight against my hand, but it was no use. It was just me, darkness and a giant freaky alien contraption in here. Since the rock I moved in front of the entry seemed to be deterring the mountain lion for the moment and there didn't seem to be anything posing any immediate danger inside the cave, I decided to wait a few moments for my eyes to adjust to the darkness before I continued to venture forward. The light outside the cave at this point was pretty much gone, as nighttime had settled into the Catalina mountainside. Hopefully, the hungry cat outside would likely give up on me and find some other delicious prey.

After a few minutes, I felt as though I could

see well enough to make it around the cave without tripping and breaking something important. Like my leg. Or my neck, for that matter.

Taking a page from my dad's book, I tried to recall the general contours of the cave itself in my mind's eye. I slowly inched my way forward on the sand, arms outstretched so as to not ram my face into anything and feeling the ground beneath my feet with every step I took. I continued until my foot struck something hard and solid.

Perfect. The cave floor.

Aside from clearly having been cut into the mountain, the ground itself felt no different than the rest of the rock in the State Park. It seemed as though someone just found this little ravine, climbed into the same hole I did with a few mining tools and dug out this nice big cavern. I couldn't begin to understand why someone would do that, but relevance changes little - the reality was that there was a humongous cave carved into the mountain and that person, or persons, decided to construct a huge metal ring in the middle of this place.

Clearly, I'm not the most savvy person, considering the mess I was in, but I do fancy myself a logical person. Logic tells me that this place was strangely secluded and hidden for one of two reasons: it's dangerous or it is valuable. Either way, I'm not sure I should have been there. Evidently, someone wanted to hide this place from... well, everybody. Being there was not likely in my best interest. Although, the large and very hungry cat still scraping at the rocks outside was definitely not in my best interest, so I figured I'd stick this one out. It's likely that whoever built this is banking on the seclusion to help hide it, so they're probably not going to be back any time soon anyway. I'd be up and out before they ever knew someone found it.

I stepped onto the cave floor and started shuffling my way toward the center of the room. After a few steps, I heard a sound like the whir of an engine starting up from the middle of the cavern. A moment later, clanking sounds and the slow chugging and screeching of gears, rumbled through the cave like a factory powering up for the first time in a while. Metal scraped across metal. I squinted in the darkness to see better but came up with nothing. I could barely see my hands in front of me, let alone several yards ahead.

The sounds grew progressively louder yet more sure and soon the grinding, clicking and chugging filling the chamber stopped and was replaced with a surprisingly steady humming symphony of machinery.

Gingerly, I took another step forward and was instantly met with blinding light from the ground beneath me. I winced, covering my eyes from the sudden light, though what had seemed intense and bright a moment earlier had quickly faded to a soft glow. I looked down and saw the ground lit with strange symbols emanating a soft blue glow. I took another step and again, was met with the same blue glow beneath my feet. Every step I took on my way toward the machine lit up a path beneath me, basking the entire room in that soft blue glow.

Being able to see helped me feel a bit more at ease about my situation, but it didn't change reality. I was still out of water, there was still a predator trying to claw its way in and I was out of food and options. Added to the mix, I was completely at a loss for understanding what I was looking at.

With the light from the ground, I could see the contraption that was taking up a sizable portion of the room. The giant metal ring was covered with designs similar to the shapes glowing on the ground all around me, except in various colors and sizes. It looked like writing. It looked Asian, but not Japanese or Chinese. When I had seen the ring with my flashlight earlier it had been resting vertically in a base. However, now that there was power, it was no longer simply resting. Instead, it was suspended in mid-air about 4 inches from the base, like one of those contraptions where a magnet rests an inch above its base using the magnetic field as a sort of invisible force. The ring was slowly rotating but gaining speed.

Above the whirring of the machine, I could hear the lion scratching at the rock guarding the entrance to the cave and giving a half-meow half-hiss. I looked back, relieved to see the cat hadn't yet gotten through my haphazard barrier and turned again to face the ring in front of me. All at once, the events of my day caught up with me and a wave of exhaustion hit me.

I plopped down next to the enormous contraption and sat facing the rock protecting me from "Mr. Cuddles" and tried to figure out a solution to my predicament. I had no water, barely any food, I was trapped in a cave by a mountain lion, and had somehow managed to stumble into some sort of weird space-age alien chamber thingy with a floating metal hula hoop spinning aimlessly. It wasn't the most relaxing vacation.

Get a plan together, Finn. You're not getting out of here by having a meltdown.

That's true. Sometimes, you have to give yourself a motivational pep talk. But people look at you funny when you talk to yourself. Thankfully, I was the only one here.

In an effort to do *something*, I scoured the room, cobbling together a few more stones in front of the entrance to reinforce my makeshift door and hopefully deter the creature outside. A short while later, the sounds from the other side of the entrance stopped altogether.

Good, maybe the lion has decided on a new creature to hunt tonight.

With nothing left to do but wait, I tried to get some rest. My pack was torn in several places, but it would make an alright pillow. I opened it up and pulled out the box of breakfast bars, dug one out of the box and settled into a delicious mouthful of oats and honey.

Hunger momentarily sated, I decided my best bet was to stay as far from the opening as I could in case the lion would broke through my fortifications, so I walked to the opposite side of the cavern. The ring floating in the middle of the room continued to rotate. I had no idea what it was supposed to do, but for the last hour or so it had only floated there, spinning quietly in circles, gaining speed until it was now moving so quickly, the colorful symbols on the edges were blending together in an array of lights. It looked a bit like those photos you can take where you leave the shutter open for a while and mess around with a flashlight or glow stick and when you finally take the picture, it looks like you've been drawing in the air with magic. Except it wasn't a picture and there was no flashlight.

I headed to the opposite end of the cave and was passing the machine to try and rest when I noticed a small bronze coin with a diamond shaped hole on the ground next to the ring. Intrigued, I stooped down to pick it up. Instantly, a piercingly loud noise kind of like an ambulance siren rang through the cave and the metal ring flashed a bright blue for just a moment.

Instinctively, I lurched backward. The ring was now blinking off and on again and the siren was blaring loudly. My mom always said my curiosity was a good thing, but it was probably going to get me in a lot of trouble. I'm thinking she was right.

Well, what have I done this time?

CHAPTER FOUR

You know that feeling you get when your stomach drops out from the bottom of your torso? Like when you're riding a roller coaster and you hit a sudden dip and you get the sense that all of your insides are about to be outsides? Well, amplify that a hundredfold and you might be in the ballpark for what was happening to me.

I slung the backpack over my shoulder and decided to get a better look at the bronze coin. The moment I moved near the metal ring, the world around me plunged to complete black and then erupted into a thousand neon colors- along the floors, the ring, the cavern walls and ceiling. At the same time, something unnatural ripped a vertical line through the air directly in front of me. The smell of burnt atmosphere blew past me and was swiftly replaced with the sterile aroma of electricity. All at once, the vertical line parted in the middle and revealed a swirling mass of blues and greens and whites twisting together while some unseen force yanked me toward this neon nightmare. White-blue streaks of electricity crackled across the surface as I came in contact with it. It felt semi-solid, like a wall of jelly, and within a moment I was forced through the barrier.

To say that I remained calm and kept my composure as all of this was occurring would be ...well, a flat out lie. As a matter of fact, after a few choice words left my mouth, I clambered and clawed to get away from this thing. I must've looked like a house cat being thrown into a bathtub. For all the flailing, I was wildly unsuccessful. As I passed through the jelly stuff, my body began to tremble and I felt as though I was being blasted with several hundred volts of electricity. It wasn't exactly painful, though I wouldn't want to experience it twice.

After passing the electrified ooze, I tumbled head over heels through some kind of a wormhole. I completely lost my sense of direction as there was nothing to hold onto. Worse yet, the horrible mass of colors continued to swirl around and past me. It was at this point that I cried out in a voice which wasn't exactly "manly." Give me some credit - there was a terrifying number of strange things happening completely out of my control and I was caught up in the moment. So sue me.

Still tumbling at an alarming rate, my mind reeled with confusion. One moment I'm deep in the Catalina mountain range, and the next I'm hurtling toward my doom through an electrified nightmare born of a Jimi Hendrix album cover art. I couldn't even begin to tell you how long I was in there. It was long enough, though, that the sensation of tumbling became somewhat commonplace and I didn't think my ears would ever regain their equilibrium. That is if I ever got out.

After what seemed like an eternity of falling, a small, bright dot of light pushed through the maze of colors ahead of me. My heart lurched at the promise of an end to this whole encounter. Then I was struck with another, altogether more terrifying notion that the light I'm seeing could be emanating from a really hard surface and, given my velocity and general inability to control my fall, that could prove painful to my poor gangly body.

As the light grew bigger and closer, I squeezed shut my eyes and braced for impact. "Please don't kill me, please don't kill me, please don't kill me" I chanted frantically to myself.

The smell of electricity and atmosphere grew intense once again and behind my closed eyelids I could tell that I was passing into the light and ...

Nothing.

I stopped moving, I stopped falling. The lights and the tunnel were gone. I didn't even jerk to a stop or anything (who says Newton knows anything about physics?). I was just there, lying on the ground in the cave.

I sat up to look around to get my bearings. Immediately, I got a head rush, my brain pounded and I was overcome with that creeping black sensation when you stand up too quickly and had to lay back down for a moment.

"This is okay. Yeah. This is okay." I said aloud.

"That....that was perfectly normal." Trying to reassure myself.

Slowly this time, I sat up and looked around. Turns out, this was definitely not the cave. Instead, I was in some sort of large warehouse, several stories tall. There were high vaulted ceilings held in place with latticed metal support beams and crosshatches. Wooden crates filled the room and bits of machinery were thrown haphazardly into piles in no recognizable order. Gears and cogs littered the floor and as I lifted my hand, a small metal sprocket stuck to my sweaty palm. The only familiar thing in the room was the same contraption from the cave. It was dormant once again, the metal ring resting gently in the base and the symbols back to the original muted colors. As a matter of fact, the entire room was completely dark, save for a small Edison bulb dangling from a long cord directly overhead.

"What the..." I managed to say before my confusion was cut short by a horrible metallic scraping sound. Instinct kicked in and I scrambled to my feet. Glancing to my left, I spotted the entrance to this room -- a large metal-plated door on an old rusted track, now slowly opening. I quickly dashed behind one of the larger crates in the corner of the room and hunkered down as best I could in such a tight spot.

Thankfully, it was dark in the corner I chose. I poked my head out from my hiding spot to see about the commotion.

"I'm telling you, the alarm was going off in

the office. Someone was down here," said a man with a high pitched, nasally voice.

"No one has been in or out of this room in months, sir," the other man said with a hint of exasperation creeping into his deep baritone voice.

"Well, it is my prerogative to check. We have some very sensitive...eh, materials...stored here and we cannot have them compromised," The first man replied as he brushed past his companion into the room.

As they stepped into the light, something struck me as very odd about both men. The man with the nasally, irritating voice was clad in dark grey britches (yes, britches) and a high waisted pea coat with long tails. His steps were accented by large black boots - the kind with flaps on the top into which his britches were tucked cleanly. His slim face was lined with age and wrinkles creased his temples where he seemed to permanently squint above the half moon glasses resting precariously at the edge of his nose. His mouth came to a sharp pucker and there was a subtle cruelty about his features. Honestly, if I hadn't been trying to hide from these guys before I saw them, his expression was enough to send me running.

In contrast, the other man with him was shorter by a head and much sturdier. He seemed to be wearing some kind of uniform, but I couldn't place it. It had an American civil-war look about it, dual-breasted with brass buttons down the front and a short, clipped collar. He was clad in all black, save for the buttons, and a sidearm was fastened to his waist. There was a small, bright red emblem on his left sleeve, but I was too far away to make it out. To me, both men seemed devastatingly out of place in terms of fashion. Then again, who am I to judge? I still cling to my over-sized tee-shirts and baggy jeans for my weekend attire.

As they walked into the light, I ducked down as far as possible while still peeking above the crate.

The shorter uniformed man urged once again, "I can assure you, Mr. Klein, that there is simply no way that anyone could get into this facility. The only entrance to the entire chamber is the same way we just came in and the lock on the outside is outfitted with triple primed, state of the art MACS. There is simply no one who can bypass those security measures."

Mr. Klein dismissed the soldier's statement outright with a wave of his hand.

"Locks can be broken. MACS can be thwarted," Klein said.

The shorter man sighed heavily, "Very well, sir, I will have a security team sweep the warehouse and the entire plaza."

"I expect as much!"

"If there was anyone who made their way back here, the culprit will be found and brought to you immediately," the shorter man continued, placing a particularly pointed amount of emphasis on the "if."

Mr. Klein took one last glance around, peering above his half-moon glasses, nodded once to himself and turned curtly on one heel to march out of the room, summarily ignoring the shorter man.

The shorter man glared at Mr. Klein as he left. I felt bad for the guy, but at the same time, it seemed that I was going to be in a heap of trouble if I didn't figure out a way to get out of this room really soon, so my compassion was short lived.

The soldier took a moment to glance around the room for himself, his eyes lingering an uncomfortably long time in my direction before he pulled a small contraption from his pocket and fidgeted with it briefly. I wasn't entirely sure from my vantage point, but it looked a bit like a smartphone with the glass screen missing. Instead, gears and motors were all exposed, and yet, he seemed to be able to get it to function.

A static sound broke the silence in the room and was replaced with a terse male voice.

"Go for Kaplan."

"Kaplan, this is Reggie," The soldier replied. Reggie?! Definitely not the name I'd have guessed. I'd have guessed maybe a Dirk. Or a Hank. Definitely not a Reggie...Reginald. Whatever.

"Yeah Reg, what's going on?" the voice on the phone thing chimed out.

Reggie held the device in an open palm and depressed a button on the side.

"Kap, there was some sort of issue with Warehouse 31. Klein was down here in a fuss about his *sensitive material* and demanding we do a sweep."

"Teams three and four are off on patrol already. Do you want them to form up?"

"Nah, there's nothing here," Reggie replied. "The locks were still active and the security system was still in place. If someone had gotten in here, they'd be completely ash by now. Since the teams are already out, can you make sure they pop by the director's office and let them know we didn't find anything?"

"Sure thing, Reg," the guy on the other end of the line relayed.

As Reggie was speaking, I was looking around for a way out. It really did seem as though I was going to need to get through that door. But how was the better question...

Looking around the room and attempting to avoid drawing any attention, I could only see the few crates and piles of scrap metal lying around.

"I'll lock up here, but I'm going to have to reset the codes, so give me two minutes to get those coded in before you re-engage the MACS," soldier Reggie chimed back.

"Affirmative. Do you want me to run the purge diagnostic?" Kaplan replied.

"It wouldn't hurt, I suppose. Give me those two minutes to head out so I don't get totally fried and then I'll contact you again."

Purge? Fried? Well, crap.

CHAPTER FIVE

I waited for Reggie to leave and the big metal door shut behind him. As soon as it closed, I dashed out from my hiding spot and frantically tried to find a way out. I searched the small windows on the far side of the room, pressing and pulling against all of the panes, but banging on the windows would probably lead to somebody noticing me, so I couldn't be too forceful. If I learned anything from that exchange between Reggie and Mr. Klein, it was pretty clear I was not supposed to be here.

None of the windows would budge. My heart raced and I could feel sweat beading on my forehead. I ran to the big door Reggie had exited and tried pulling, but he must have locked it because I wasn't able to open it. I ran around the room trying to find any floor vents or air ducts that I could climb into to get out, but everything was either too high up or blocked. A moment later an ear piercing siren began whirring away and a red light began flashing above the door.

No no no, I muttered frantically. *I don't know what is about to happen but it can't be good!*

Scared and out of options, I began banging on the door, hoping that somebody would realize that there was a person in here and stop whatever they were initiating. At the same time, two holes on either side of the doorway opened on the floor and two black, strange pillars started to rise. They ascended up all the way to the ceiling and a moment later began lighting up. I couldn't tell you what the heck was going on, but I certainly didn't want to be near those things when whatever was about to happen happened. I retreated back to the metal ring and cowered down behind it in hopes that I'd be able to hide from the purge.

The sirens continued to get louder and louder and more lights began flashing in the room until the two pillars lit up from top to bottom with a bright blue light that literally started *seeping* from the pillars. They looked like tall circular LED lamps with a weird neon blue tint which emanated outward like a slowly expanding balloon or bubble. Oh, and the bubble had streaks of electricity or lightning or something zipping around in it. Yeah, so *that* was happening.

As the light reached out through the room, everything it came in contact with was swallowed by the blue glow and if it wasn't metal and nailed to the ground, it was instantly disintegrated. It didn't matter if it was a box, some lint or dust, cobwebs or the paper hanging on the wall near the door (I think it was some sort of shipping manifest or something). Absolutely everything touched by the light was systematically dismantled.

To say that I was scared would mean I had enough time to process exactly what was happening. The course of events probably took no more than 10 seconds for the room to be enveloped by this blue purging light. To me, though, it seemed like the light was seeping out at a slow and painfully molasses-like rate. Maybe my body wanted to just savor the moment and let me remember that I was going to die by electrified ooze bubble. I squeezed my eyes shut and waited for it to all be over.

I sure know how to take a relaxing weekend off of work, huh? Being stupid enough to forget to pack enough water to begin with, and then getting chased by a mountain lion, barricaded into a cave, sucked into some weird interdimensional portal thingy, hiding from armed guards and now about to be vaporized by a blue aura of doom. Maybe next time I can go skydiving without a parachute.

All right, maybe that's a little dark, but I am, after all, the one who's about to be molecularised by a weird sci-fi laser blob.

Behind my eyelids, I could see the light getting brighter and I knew it was only moments away. Just then, I heard a ripping sound, that distinct smell of burnt ozone and my heart lurched. I peeled open my eyes and I saw the portal was open again.

I didn't waste any time. I dove head-first into the weird gelatinous barrier between me and the nauseating colors in the portal. Once again, a shock jolted my body as I made contact with the ooze, but at least this time I was prepared for it. I braced against the blow and surprisingly, it didn't hurt as bad the second time. I tumbled head over heels and hoped beyond hope that it would spit me back out in the cave. At least there, I'd only be eaten by a really hungry desert predator.

The time I spent in that portal went by a lot faster the second time. Within moments, that same bright light appeared and I braced for impact. White radiance engulfed me and in an instant, I was flung from the portal.

Instead of being on the ground in the cave or back in the warehouse, this time, I was falling helplessly through the open sky above an absolutely massive city. And as if things haven't already been *just peachy*, in about 10 seconds, I was about to splat into a shower of Finn bits all over the ground.

CHAPTER SIX

When I was 18, my buddies and I decided it would be a fantastic idea to go out to the middle of nowhere in Idaho and prove our manliness. How you say? We decided that we would pay someone to allow us to jump out of their perfectly good airplane. So we went skydiving and, truthfully, it was a blast. The fear and excitement got my adrenaline going and the moment when I put my foot out the door of a moving plane without any ground beneath me for several thousand feet is unlike any experience I've ever had. The wind rushed all around and for a few moments, I felt like I was truly flying. Then, just pull the cord on the parachute, all that momentum stops and I calmly glided down to the earth. The experience is serene.

It's completely silent, save for the sound of the wind breezing past. The whole experience is incredibly peaceful as you enjoy unbroken views.

The mind-numbing freefall to my untimely death I was currently experiencing was definitely *not* peaceful. The ground was rapidly approaching and I was gaining momentum every second. I didn't know what to do. There was nothing to grab and nothing to slow me down. Nothing. My mind was racing and my heart was pounding so fast it probably would've won the Indy 500.

I tried to orient myself somehow to stop spinning. The more I tried, the more I found it is a lot harder to do than the professional skydivers make it look. In all the falling, twisting and turning, I spotted something in the air a ways off and rocketing through the air headed toward me.

A moment later, I was hit by something hard and sharp, felt an intense pop in both my chest and arm and promptly blacked out.

н·н·н·н·н·н·н

I don't know how long I was unconscious. As I awoke, my head pounded and my whole body felt like it weighed six tons. Something pressed hard against me and I realized that I was face down on a table like a massage therapist has, where there's a special hole for your face so you don't suffocate. I opened my eyes and tried to flip onto my back and regretted my choice at once. First off, I found out that my arms and legs were tied down. Immediately, sharp pains shot through my entire left side, shoulder to foot, and it felt as though my body had been dipped in liquid fire. My vision went black with the pain and I decided it wasn't so bad to just stay put. As long as I wasn't moving, nothing really hurt. Breathing seemed okay. I could feel my limbs and I tried wiggling my fingers. Naturally, panic set in once again and I started to freak out.

"Hehhlo," I called out.

"Whaaa ahhhm meh?" I mumbled into the table. I don't think my mouth was working. Or my brain, for that matter. I took a breath and tried to shake off some of the drowsiness.

A cold, firm hand pressed on my upper back and a gruff male voice spoke.

"Don't move. If you move, you'll die."

Well, that is a refreshing turn of events. Good thing I haven't reached my quota for near-death experiences yet today.

"Seriously," the man continued, "I just spent the last 19 hours putting you back together and I am not about to have my work undone because you move and jolt the augs out of place."

The what?

His voice was rigid but sincere and I could tell he was irritated. He had an unmistakable English accent.

"Nihntheen 'ous," I stammered. "Whaeh ahm ehy?"

It felt like my tongue wouldn't work or was too thick for my mouth, and everything in my mind was moving like molasses.

"Nineteen and a few minutes, by the dragon's tail," he remarked, still holding his hand solidly in the spot between my shoulder blades. "The name is Giles. And you, young lad, are lucky to be alive."

"Luckhy toh be ahliveh? Ehy don evhn knoh whaas goin ohn," each word was a serious effort of will to produce and came out thick and awkward.

"Yes sir," he said, easing slightly his pressure on my back. "I have no idea how you got up there, but my daughter and a few others saw you falling and ran over to where you were. They weren't able to stop you from hitting the ground but a few of the boys managed to throw something together to break the fall. Seems they weren't the only ones to notice you. The Hand must've thought you were something hostile since they sent that Curator at you. You're lucky you weren't closer to the city or there'd have been nothing left of you to hit the ground!"

I felt something firm pulling on me, a twinge of pain in my lower back and ribs and then Giles' took his hand off my back.

"Now son, don't move. Eva and the boys may have stopped you from smashing into the ground, but you were still badly hurt. Doctor Bardell was able to stop the bleeding and stabilize you, but he knew that you needed intense reconstruction to survive. Eva called me and I brought everything I could think of that might help."

I took a deep breath again and winced, trying to ignore the pain ripping through my side I worked to speak more clearly. Giles was patient as I huffed out a few awkward sounds until I got the words out.

"I dohn't unnnder-ssstand," I muttered through gritted teeth. "I don't even know how I got here. Orhh where *here* even is!" The words came out more clearly but they were labored and difficult.

My mind was clearing up and I was slowly starting to process what had happened. Being tied face down on a table in a stranger's house, unable to move or even look around wasn't helping matters, either. I felt heat rushing to my face and my heart beat quickly. I wanted to punch something. I wanted to run as far away from here as I could. In all honesty, I was downright angry. What the crap happened to me?

"Settle down, settle down. Can't have you pulling something if you get all worked up," Giles said. I could hear him fidgeting with something off to my left.

"You're upset and I understand that. So let's begin with the basics. This is my shop, for starters," Giles stated matter of fact. "Fleming Gildwares. And we're in the Etherborough Ward. You've likely not been this way much. We're in 8-9 and almost off of the Embervein." The way he said it sounded like "eight dash nine" and meant every word of what he said.

"I must've really rahttlled my brain because nothing you said made ehhny sense," I said and then cleared my throat. "I'm from Tucson. In the

US. Is this England or something?"

"Hmph. I'm not familiar with that area. Maybe you're a bit confused. You did hit your head really hard. But then again, these Wards keep growing and trying to take every little bit of space they possibly can and I can't keep up with them all."

"No, *you* don't understand!" I blurted out, nearly yelling into the table. "One minute, I was out for a hike. The next, I'm almost being 'purged' by some weird blue laser light show."

I couldn't help it, I was frustrated and nothing made sense. I pulled at my restraints on the table and I felt heat rising in my chest and face.

"And *then*," I said as I yanked with my wrists, "I'm plummeting to my death over some gigantic city, only to smash into little bits and put back together by Dr. Frankenstein!"

I was met with silence.

A moment passed and still Giles said nothing.

"Well?!" I called out, my voice cracking slightly.

Silence.

I knew he was still there because I could hear him breathing slowly behind me, but he refused to say anything. Face down on this table unable to move, I sucked in a few short steadying breaths and allowed my rage to die down. After all, it wasn't this guy's fault that I had a really messed up day. I sighed, frustrated at myself for letting my temper get away from me and winced in pain as I tried to take a deep breath.

"Giles?" I said, turning my head to look toward him. The moment I moved even an inch, a burning sensation abruptly shot through my body and forced me to freeze until the pain subsided.

It was silent a moment longer and then Giles cleared his throat.

"I'm sorry, boy. It's clear that you've had quite the ordeal. We can look into what you said, but for now, there are more pressing issues for us to discuss," He said as he walked around to my right side, rested his hand gently on my shoulder and squatted down next to me as he spoke.

"I need to talk with you about your situation."

Oh boy. That's never a good sign. I felt my pulse pick up tempo once again.

"When you fell, a Curator was sent out and managed to clip your left side. It broke your arm in several places, along with a few ribs and your femur," he said as he took a deep breath. I got a sinking feeling that he was steeling himself for more bad news.

"I wish that were the worst of it, but it isn't. As you landed, those boys were able to slow you down a bit, but the human body just isn't designed to take such a beating. You hit the ground at an alarming speed and it jarred your entire body. You're bruised all over and in a few places, your skin split open. Doctor Bardell was able to help with that, but the worst part was your spine. You hit the ground and basically folded in half. Seven of your vertebrae in your lower back were simply reduced to bone dust. They splintered into dozens of pieces each and your spinal column was mangled beyond repair."

My breath caught in my mouth and I felt the blood drain from my whole body.

"But..." I stammered. It couldn't be true, could it? I had been moving my hands, my feet, my arms. I couldn't help it. I tend to talk with my hands. But if what he said is accurate, then how was that even possible? Shouldn't I be paralyzed? Or dead?

"Allow me to finish," Giles interjected, his hand on my shoulder squeezing just a touch to draw my focus back to him. "It seems as though things here are unfamiliar to you. Maybe that is a result of memory loss due to your fall or maybe it is something else, so let me explain a bit of what I do for a living. I am an Aesthesium surgeon. My job is to implant workable Augs into people who have been injured or in some way have lost the use of various parts of their body. I work alongside doctors and medical staff to bring about quality of life improvements due to physical malformation. Typically, this is either creating part of an arm or leg or maybe a few fingers or toes. But every so often, there are more extreme cases where I need to replace part of a torso or entire limbs or even internal organs."

He ran a hand through his hair and continued, "Working on you, though, was one of the most intense and difficult procedures I've ever had to do. I haven't had to create a spine before and so I cobbled together your replacement from other pieces I brought with me. Ultimately, I think I got you back together but we won't know for sure for a few weeks whether or not you'll regain mobility or even sensations throughout your body."

He paused a moment. It felt like forever...

I could *feel* my body. I could feel my arms,

legs, back and everything else. It was there! I could feel it!

Giles must've known what I was thinking because he nodded his head, seemingly to himself and spoke up.

"Clearly, some of the reconstruction was successful, since your arms have some mobility, but I wouldn't press your luck. You don't want to rip out any of the sutures or further injure anything. Try to avoid talking with your hands as much as possible and only small, gentle motions if you must."

He continued, "It is going to be very painful for a very long time, but I will help you through it. It's going to take a lot of work to make sure that you are able to walk and function again. Probably several months or even a year, by the dragon's tail."

I didn't have the words for what I was feeling. My whole life was turned upside down in the span of a few minutes. And now this guy is telling me that I might never walk again?

"I…" I trailed off. A lump was caught in my throat and my entire body seemed to lock up. I tried to form the words to what I was feeling but it was too painful to even think about it.

Giles quietly continued, "It's alright. You

don't need to speak right now. I'm going to go get some food and we'll start with making sure you're fed." There was hope in his voice. The edginess was gone, replaced with a concern that I didn't expect.

"By the way, I have a feeling we're going to be seeing a lot of each other for a while and it'd be a shame to call you 'boy' for the entire time. Can you recall your name?"

My mouth and throat were dry and it was still extremely difficult to form the words.

"Finn. My name is Finn Riley," I managed to say.

"Mmmm, Finn, then," he replied, mulling the words over as he spoke. "Let me get us some food, and then you should rest."

He stood up and dusted off his hands. He turned to a table nearby and messed with something and soon after, I heard him walk away and a door closed somewhere off to my left.

I laid there motionless and soaked in what Giles had told me. The notion that I might never walk again terrified me.

I didn't ask for this.

I still couldn't imagine how any of this happened. You think you know what you're doing and how life is going to play out, and in the blink of an eye everything gets thrown away. All I wanted was a quiet weekend out in the mountains so I could reorient myself from a crappy job. Sure, maybe I should have been a bit more prepared with my supplies, but *this*? There is no way I could have planned for this. And now it's going to cost me at least a year of my life to get back to "normal," whatever that is.

In any case, maybe it was the sheer scope of the trauma or the fact that I had been operated on for over nineteen hours, but moments after Giles left the room, exhaustion flooded my system. My body gave up and I passed out once again.

CHAPTER SEVEN

As I came to again, I found myself somewhere new. At least I think it was new since the last thing I saw was some sort of workshop mixed with a medical office. I was lying on my back now, facing a large room which looked to be a bedroom of sorts, though not quite like any bedroom I've been in before. For starters, it was absolutely *massive*. Looking around it seemed more like a ballroom than a bedroom, save for the huge four-poster bed I was lying on. The floors were a sandy brown polished marble. The walls mimicked the floors, made of a stone that had been smoothed to a polished finish. There were only a few windows and very little light was coming in from the outside. I couldn't tell if it was night time or not but it was dark outside. There was a small table with some antique chairs, though they didn't have that worn out look that is typical of most antique furniture.

Near the sitting area was a large fireplace which had clearly seen some use recently, as soot and dirt lined both the fireplace and the hearth surrounding it. Other than that, the room was fairly barren. I tried to sit up, but just as before, shooting pains ripped through my back.

I glanced down and saw myself bandaged from my neck all the way down my chest. Someone had dressed me in light robe and the blankets covered everything else. I could only assume that I was probably wrapped head to toe based on what Giles said the other day. My muscles ached and I had no desire to repeat that explosion of pain, so I just simply lay there, staring at the empty room, wishing that I could just go back home.

Since I was in no position to move around, it gave me a chance to think. I had no idea how long it had been since I was dropped into this strange place and I had no idea how to get back. I don't know what happened to open that portal and I definitely do not know *why on earth* it kept happening. I felt heat rising to my face with the thought of never seeing my home again, let alone never walking again.

It wasn't going to do me any good to have a full blown panic attack, so I worked on slowing my breathing and trying to figure out the next steps. First things first, I needed to figure out where I was. Once I figured that out, then perhaps I could find someone who knew something about how those portals work and perhaps they would help me figure out a way back home. It seems to me that if I could fall through a freaky portal then I'm probably not the only one, right? No one is *that* special.

My thoughts were interrupted as the large door on the opposite end of the room opened with a click and a thud. A small woman with brown curly hair that fell to her shoulders came bustling into the room with a tray in her hands. She was slightly overweight, wearing a brown and white dress covered by a lace trimmed apron and she seemed a bit clumsy. Plates and silverware clinked and rattled on the tray as she struggled to open the door, trying not to spill what she was carrying. She looked up from the tray to where I was lying and her eyes lit up. Seeing that I was awake, she hurried towards the bed and a grin pulled at the edges of her cheeks.

"Oh mister Finn, I'm so glad to see you are awake!" she said as she made her way across the massive room.

"My name is Gladys Weatherby and I work here for Dr. Fleming. He had you moved here to the guest quarters when you didn't wake up for any food. He said your skin was still very fragile, but seemed to be taking to the sutures and he thought it was safe to move you. I hope that is alright."

She bustled over to the bedside and set down the tray filled with different bowls of soup and a few small loaves of bread with small dishes of jellies and spreads to go with them.

"Is there anything that you need or desire, young man? It's my job to make sure that any of Dr. Fleming's guests are taken care of." Her voice was bubbly and laced with a slight British accent, but had that weathered tone that comes with age.

"Uhh, no, I think I'm okay for now." My throat was dry and the words came out coarse and chopped. I had to swallow several times to get through the entire sentence.

"Very well, my dear. But just so you know, if you need anything, you can get ahold of me on the Messorium." She smiled and turned to walk away.

"Wait," I said quickly. She turned and arched an eyebrow in my direction.

"What's a Messorium?" I asked sheepishly.

Her mouth opened slightly and I could see she was surprised by the question. Her eyebrows furled and unfurled as she processed the thought.

"Ah, yes, well Mr. Fleming did say you might have some memory loss." She brushed her hands across the front of her apron to smooth out the wrinkles, an action that seemed more like a thinking mannerism than a necessary one and continued.

"The Messorium is that little device there on the table there," she stated, pointing to the nightstand next to the bed. Sure enough, a small metal box that looked like a smartphone without a screen sat idly against the base of a lamp, just like what I had seen in the warehouse earlier.

"It serves as our primary communication device. It enables one to communicate across long distances. Most people use it for speaking, but it can also be used to send written messages as well."

It was my turn to arch an eyebrow. "So a cell phone, then?"

Gladys cocked her head to the side and gave me an entirely puzzled look.

"I'm sorry? I'm not familiar..." her voice trailed off and she shook her head and resumed her previous smiling, cheerful look.

"Anyway, just press on the green button, let the monitor know who you would like to speak to and you'll be ahold of me in no time. You can also reach Dr. Fleming this way as well, or anyone else you may like to contact if you have family or friends who might be missing you right now. They would be welcome to come by and see you."

She smiled and turned once again to leave.

I interjected again, "Do you know how long it has been since my accident?"

Without missing a beat, Gladys turned deliberately on a heel to face me.

"Thirteen days, young man." Every word was dramatically emphasized and her eyes were wide. She was clearly shaken by the thought.

"Thirteen days?!" I blurted out.

"If it weren't for the fact that you were still breathing, I would've thought you dead!" she exclaimed, her eyebrows rising high on her forehead. "Oh mister Finn, I don't know you, really. But a young man with his life ahead of him broken into little pieces and put back together again? I'm heartbroken for you!"

She ran her hands over her apron again.

"And *then*," she continued dramatically as if she was the one who was actually injured, "I was worried you had lapsed into some sort of coma. I kept coming in with food and making sure you were at least comfortable, but even when we moved you in here, you didn't stir one bit!"

Her features rumpled and she grabbed the edges of her apron.

"I just…" she stammered as she drew a hand up to her mouth, tears welling in her eyes.

I interrupted and gave her the best smile I could muster.

"Well, I don't think I did. And thank you for taking such good care of me. I don't deserve your hospitality. Or your help, for that matter. Like you said, you don't even know me."

It took her a moment to compose herself, but she let go of her apron, smoothing it out once more and smiled back. "Young man, we may not be like the rest of Emberwall, but a person in need is always welcome here. And you are *certainly* in need."

I didn't want to make her any more worked

up than she already was so I refrained from asking her any more questions, even though each time she spoke, more and more questions flooded my mind.

She took a deep breath and let out a satisfied huff. "Well, then. Do you need any help to eat this afternoon?"

I tried lifting an arm and found it unpleasant, but not unbearable. It'd apparently been nearly two weeks since I'd moved my joints so I wanted to give them a little exercise.

"I'll try and manage. If I need help, you'll be the first to know," I said, smiling gratefully.

"Enjoy the soup, then, and let me know if you have any other needs," Gladys said as she walked back across the room and shut the door behind her.

As soon as she left, I let out a sigh. This place seemed so normal on the outside, the little bits I've had a chance to see, yet every time I spoke to someone, it got more and more bizarre. Who doesn't know what a cell phone is? And what is Emberwall? What is an Aesthesium surgeon? And how did he fix my back and side? That kind of reconstruction should have been impossible and yet here I sit, and as long as I don't really move that much, I'm not in any real pain. Heck, the fact that I can *move* is a downright miracle. None of this should even be possible.

Thankfully, the food looks normal. The bedroom is extravagant, but it's decently normal. The people seem normal, although Gladys' getup looked a bit archaic. She looked more like a nursemaid from the 1800s than a personal assistant or aide to a physician.

Lost in my thoughts, a loud growling, squealing sound jolted me back to reality. Glancing down, I realized my stomach made that awful noise. If I really hadn't eaten for thirteen days, I'm pretty certain I should be dead. Or at least unable to move. Maybe I had been hooked up to some kind of IV tap or something. Anyway, I slowly and gingerly reached over to the tray that Gladys had left at my bedside and tried some soup.

Perhaps it was the fact that I was literally starving, but I can tell you here and now - that was the *best* soup I've ever had in my life. It was savory and creamy and hearty all at the same time. I couldn't even tell you what was in it, but each spoonful, as slow and painful as it was to move my arm, was a welcome sip of warm heaven.

CHAPTER EIGHT

I enjoyed my soup in silence until a quiet knock thumped at the door.

"Come in!" I called out across the obnoxiously large room while I slurped down the last of the soup, tilting the bowl to my mouth with my good hand.

The door cracked open once more and a young lady popped her head in. It was genuinely hard to make out any distinguishing features of anyone from that distance, but what struck me first was her alarmingly bright red hair.

"I heard you were awake and I wanted to come to say hello," she said as she slipped in the doorway and shut the door behind her.

"Hello," I said, looking over the bowl at my

mouth. At once, I had to catch my breath. The young lady moved with deliberate confidence as she closed the distance from the door to my bed. She was slender, but not weak. She was maybe 21 years old and had red hair that gently curled and flowed down to the middle of her back. She wore a dark green jacket with toggles across the front that parted at her waist and flowed out behind her as she walked. Her pants were a dark brown and she wore several belts around her waist. Several tools rest at her hips but I couldn't tell what they were or what they did.

She quickly made her way across the room. As she did, it dawned on me that I was staring at her and took a moment to compose myself.

"My name is Eva."

"Hello," I repeated, still holding the bowl to my mouth.

Yep. I'm a real charmer. Nice going, Finn.

"Your name is Finn, right?" She sat down on a chair nearby to the bed and leaned toward me.

She didn't come across nearly as formal as Gladys had shortly before and while she also seemed to have an accent, it wasn't as defined or astute sounding as Gladys or Giles.

"Mmhmm, yeah that's right," I said as I

lowered the bowl and set it on the tray next to me. "You're the one who saved me, right?"

"Well, I was the one who saw you falling, but Trent, Harris, and Lucky were the ones who stopped you from smashing into the ground," she said, adjusting her tools as she got comfortable.

"Well, thank you," I said, trying to sound as genuine as I could. "Seriously, thank you. I feel horrible and can't move most of my body without pain shooting throughout my entire core, but I would be, ya know, *dead* if it weren't for you and your friends."

Eva sat back and folded her arms across her chest and her expression was flat.

Uhh. So, maybe I should work on that. Sarcasm probably wasn't the best way to express my appreciation.

"Yeah. You're right. You *would* be dead," she shot back, her tone colder than before. "And my dad spent the last two weeks making sure that you can even open that mouth of yours, so you should be grateful."

If I was physically capable of shying away, I would have been cowering. I changed tactics.

"Uh. No, I'm sorry. I didn't mean for that to come out the way it did. I really am grateful and

I really do appreciate all that you and your family have done for me. I don't deserve your kindness, let alone your dad's giving of time and skills for me."

Eva relaxed a bit and ran a hand through her hair, glancing down at the ends as her hand mindlessly messed with one of her curls.

"Yeah. Well, you're welcome," she said quietly.

"Let me try again," I said, straightening up in bed as best I could without wincing in pain.

"Hi. My name is Finn. I'm from Tucson. Thank you so much for your kindness and hospitality." I smiled and gingerly stuck out a hand.

A few beats passed before she rolled her eyes, sighed and shook my hand. There was an awkward pause afterward and we just sat there in silence.

Finally, she cleared her throat and asked, "So, uh. How did you get up there, anyway? I mean, in the sky, earlier. When I saw you fall. It's like you just appeared there."

"I have no idea," I replied frankly. "I don't really remember the last few weeks, but that day is burned into my brain."

I told her the story of what had happened to me, best as I was able to recall. As I spoke, she leaned forward, her head resting on her hand, her legs crossed and her eyes locked on me.

Periodically, she interrupted and asked questions.

"What Ward is Tucson in? I haven't heard of it before. It must be near the mountain if you were hiking."

"Well, it's near the Catalina mountain range, but it's nowhere near this city. I don't even know where we are. Tucson is in Arizona. It's a desert, but, ya know, at least 'it's a dry heat'," I said, waiting for the obligatory chuckle that usually follows that phrase. Eva's expression remained blank, so I shook my head and continued on with my story.

A few minutes later, she interrupted again, "Wait, so you were attacked by a beast? That isn't even possible! There hasn't been a sighting of any sort of creature like that in generations!"

"Well, I doubt that," I replied. "People see them all the time. But you try to stay away from them for obvious reasons."

Her eyes grew wide with excitement. "Wow, well I need to get out more!"

"Perhaps, but don't go looking for a mountain lion. They'll just tear you to shreds."

I continued my story, telling of the portal to that weird warehouse factory with Mr. Klein and Reggie.

"Wait," she interjected, leaning even further forward in her chair while clapping her hands down on her knees. "Do you mean to tell me you were in Blackfort?!"

"Uhh, no? Yes? I don't know what that is…" I replied.

"Blackfort?" she said again, gesturing up in the air with her hands with all sort of shapes supposedly to help me guess whatever she was talking about.

"You know, the top defense center in the entire city? They occupy 4 levels of the Netherward and literally no one is allowed over there unless you work for the Hand," she said incredulously, as if this was just casual knowledge.

"Ohhhhhkaayyy, then sure. Yeah. That's where I was..." I shrugged as best I was able. I continued, describing the outfit Reggie was wearing and her eyes lit up again.

"That sounds like the private security teams from Netherward all right."

I nodded along, but even as she spoke, questions were already bouncing into my mind and I was hungry for answers.

"Tell you what, let me finish and then maybe I can ask you some questions, if thats ok?"

"Yeah, sure!" She was clearly excited by the entire story and had shifted to sit cross legged on the chair, as close to the edge of the bed as possible, her knee next to the tray of empty dishes.

I explained the purge sequence and then falling through the air above the city.

"By the Ember," she breathed out excitedly. "You mean to tell me that you opened not two Lusynos portals, snuck into the most fortified defense system in the city and you didn't even know what you were doing?!"

"Uh, I guess so?" I said, still completely confused as to what was going on.

Do you ever have those moments when someone is way more excited about something than you and you just don't get it? That was me right now. To Eve, I had clearly accomplished some sort of amazing feat but I had no idea how or why.

"I just want to know how to reverse it and go home, honestly," I said.

I think she missed what I said because she

grabbed my hand and squeezed it tightly, her eyes alight and a smile pulling at the furthest edges of her cheeks. I got the feeling that she could barely contain herself right now.

"This is *amazing*," she nearly squealed. "You're a Lusynosian! There hasn't been a natural born Lusynosian in generations!"

"A what?" I replied, confusion etching my face.

"A *Lusynosian*," she replied more emphatically, like that was somehow going to help me understand it better.

"No, no, I heard that. But what is that?"

"You can't be serious," she said, her expression changing slightly and she seemed disappointed that I had asked the question.

We seemed to have some rapport growing and I didn't want my ignorance to stifle the conversation. I needed her to help me understand what was going on here and why on earth I had ended up in this strange place so I pressed onward through her hesitation.

"Okay, hang on to that thought, Eva. I think I need to work through a few questions before you write me off as some total crazy guy who apparently lives in a box."

She nodded slightly, squeezed my hand gently and then returned hers to her lap and replied, "Okay, I think that's a good idea."

"Let's begin with the assumption that I'm not from here," I offered.

"But if...," she started, but I continued, ignoring her protests.

"*Because* to be truthful, I don't have any idea about anything you, your dad or anyone has been talking about. Emberwall, Blackfort, Lusynos? I don't know what those are. And your dad said he was some kind of 'Aesthesium' surgeon? What is that? Obviously it's like some sort of bioengineer but I've been in school for a while and never once heard of something like that."

Eva leaned back in her chair though she faced my direction. She nodded along as I spoke, but I could tell she was confused, trying to work through the thought of someone *genuinely* not being from this place. The whole time, she stared intently at me and rarely blinked. If I could have moved, trust me I would have. Her bright blue eyes were intense, and combined with her striking red hair and lean frame, it felt like she was peering into my soul.

Several moments passed before she

took a deep breath and seemed to have come to some sort of conclusion.

"Okay," she said, dropping her hands to her knees and pulling herself forward. "I believe you."

Yay. Now I just have to convince her Santa isn't real, and we'll be all set.

Just then, a sound like a bird chirping came from her pocket and Eva pulled out a small square box, nearly identical to the one on the nightstand near my bed. A messorium. She pushed the button on the side and reached up to her ear. I hadn't noticed it before, probably because her hair was covering it, but on her left ear, she wore a cuff which looked like a mix between a hearing aid and a bluetooth headset. A metal frame rested in her inner ear and laced around the top of her ear, hooking around to the outside of her ear and cuffing onto the cartilage of her ear.

As she held her hand to her ear, her expression changed again and a scowl crossed her features. A moment later, she pressed the same button and replaced the device in her pocket.

"I'm sorry, Finn. I need to go. My dad needs me in the workshop," she said apologetically. Quickly, she gathered herself and climbed off the chair.

"It was really nice to officially meet you and I'll be back soon. We'll talk more and I'll try to help you figure things out."

"Oh, ok. Yeah that's fine. I'm not going anywhere anyway," I said, gesturing around me playfully. Eva smiled a small but reassuring smile and then quickly left.

I sighed heavily and looked around.

My mind was brimming with questions, more now than ever. I still didn't really know anything about where I was and started to get the feeling that this wasn't just a weird trip to a foreign country (go figure, huh?). Everyone I'd met sounded relatively normal and they spoke English, but there was definitely nothing normal about this place. The portal dropped me somewhere that wasn't where I left and there was no telling where this was. It sounded so stupid to even say "the portal dropped me," like that was a *totally natural* thing to happen.

Thankfully, the people were nice and I was still alive and breathing. That had to account for something, right? Then again, I was talking myself into believing portals and trippy sci-fi dimensional travel.

I decided that maybe I should just shut my

eyes and let my body sink into the pillows in an attempt to get some rest. Oddly enough, I found it less difficult to shut off my brain than I expected. I allowed the tension to seep from my muscles and reached for the promise of sleep behind my eyes.

Just then, a sudden and excruciatingly loud bang pierced the silence and the entire room shook violently. The tray next to me rattled, slid and smashed to the ground. At once, the world plunged into complete darkness.

CHAPTER NINE

My eyes snapped open. I clung to the bedspread and tried to stabilize myself, but as shaking continued, it was so violent that it sent pain rippling out from my spine across my entire body in agonizing waves of what I can only describe as little bits of death. The lights in the room had gone out and any light coming in from outside had also been snuffed out. I couldn't see anything and I felt as though I was going to pass out from the pain.

After a few moments, the shaking subsided and an eerie silence fell upon the whole of my world. In the blackness, all I heard was my labored breathing as I strained to hear if anything was happening outside my room.

"Hello?!" I yelled frantically. "What was

that?!"

As I called out, pain ripped through my ribcage and I gasped at the sudden pain. I bit my lip and took a second to breathe and remain calm, but make no mistake - I was freaking out. Tucson isn't known for its earthquakes and this was the first time I'd ever been in something like this. My heart was pounding in my chest and the pain was still cascading through my torso and limbs with growing intensity.

I fumbled around on the bed for the cell phone thing that Gladys had left me, but it wasn't where I remembered.

I waited a moment for my eyes to adjust to the darkness. Several seconds later, shapes began taking form around me. I squinted and looked around to try to find the Messorium, but couldn't make out much in the permeating darkness. Silence completely enveloped the room and the blackness had a disquieting feel. A shiver slid up my spine and I shrugged it off as I continued searching for the Messorium. After a few more moments of scanning the shapes around the room, I spotted it. In all of the shaking, it must have fallen off the bed and slid across the room a few feet.

I called out once again, "Can anyone hear

me!? Is anyone there?"

Silence responded in kind.

This is fine. This is totally normal. I bet this happens here all the time! They're probably used to this by now and are all just enjoying some food and coffee and just forgot to let me know that this was something that happened at doomsday o'clock each day. Yeah. That's probably what it is.

A moment later, I heard a loud click and then a voice in the darkness. It sounded like a 1920s commercial on the radio.

"Citizens of Emberwall, please proceed indoors. The Proterezar is in session. The Arcmagus will protect us. The Hand will be in the streets to investigate and enforce. For your safety, do not go outside. Do not open the door to anyone. A yellow alert curfew is in effect." And then there was silence. Another loud click chimed, and the message repeated.

Okay, if I was confused before, I think dumbfounded or completely stupefied would be more accurate at this point. Perhaps a bit paranoid, too. I tried calling out again to see if anyone could hear me but I was once again met with nothing but silence and the evaporating hope that anyone would arrive to fill me in on the situation. The darkness continued and no sound came from outside.

Time passed painfully slowly and though I periodically called out in the darkness, I felt more and more alone. The more I sat there, the more I realized the predicament I was in. I didn't know where I was and I had no way of getting ahold of anyone, and I was pretty much unable to move from my spot on the bed. Time was passing way too slowly and I felt as though no one was going to come and get me. Worse yet, that message sounding out in the darkness gave me no comfort that *safety* was in my immediate future. I knew what I needed to do.

I reached over and grabbed one of the many pillows on the bed, moving slowly as to not incur any more jolts of pain in my attempts to move my limbs. I took the cover off of the pillow and rolled it up into a tube shape, like a bandanna, and gingerly tied it around my mouth behind my head. I took a deep breath in through my nose and bit down on the cloth.

With a heave, I pulled myself by my arms to the side of the bed. My vision burst with agonizing pains and I felt like I was dipping my body into a vat of burning coals. Heat and pain seared across my back, my arms and my legs. My chest felt heavy and every moment was a battle to try and simply breathe. I let out a scream, muffled by my makeshift gag, and I bit down hard on the cloth. I pulled myself forward to the edge of the bed. Getting down off the bed was going to be a new adventure in pain and I knew it. Sweat beaded on my forehead and coated my hair. With another heave, I pulled forward and slid off the bed, minimizing the pressure and pain as best I could. I bit down on the pillowcase and allowed myself a moment to breathe, composing myself for the next part. I felt lightheaded and my vision faded in and out from the pain. I don't remember, but I'm pretty sure I passed out for a moment when I hit the floor.

Pain washed over me. I felt something cold and sticky under my robe, but couldn't look down. Perhaps it was good that it was pitch black in the room. At least I didn't have to look at my own mangled body. I bit down even harder on the cloth and pulled myself forward across the floor, squeaking against the polished marble. I could see the Messorium lying a few feet away and I had to get it. Every moment I spent on the floor was a new adventure in pain, and yet externally, I could feel very little. My legs and my torso had gone numb and I was seriously worried I had just paralyzed myself. Or worse.

What had seemed like an eternity to get across the floor had probably only been a few seconds, but I finally clawed my way over to the Messorium, spit out my makeshift gag and pressed the little button on the side like I had seen done before.

"Hello?" I wept into the machine. "I need help. Please..." I was sobbing and in so much pain that I doubt the words were coherent.

"Gladys? Eva? Giles?"

Silence.

"Is anyone out there? I need help." My voice was weak and my breathing was labored. All I met was silence.

Under my arms and chest, the ground was wet and I was scared that it might be blood or my bowels. A sense of helplessness washed over me. Sweat dripped down my head and face and mixed with my tears. My body shook of its own accord. I was pretty sure the stitches in my left arm had split open because blood now trickled through the bandage down my wrist and onto the floor. The pain shredding my entire body was so massive, I simply passed out.

Some time later, and I really couldn't tell you how long that was, I awoke. It was still dark and deathly silent in the room. My face and arms were wet and sticky and my body felt heavy. As I came to, I heard the latch on the door click. The heavy metal frame squeaked as the door open slightly and a dim yellow light cut through the darkness. I heard the door close once again, and quiet footfalls on the marble floor echoing across the room.

"Finn, it's me," a familiar voice called out quietly. I squinted, and a moment later I could see Eva's shape moving towards me, her light panning around the room. She seemed hurried and out of breath.

"Eva..." I breathed out. I don't know why but I felt compelled to whisper at this point. Maybe it's because it has been dark for a few minutes or because I was pretty sure there was something scary going on outside. Most likely, it was because I could barely breathe and using my vocal cords took more energy than I really had at this point.

" By the Ember!" Eva muttered under her breath when she reached me on the floor. She kneeled down and quickly surveyed the situation.

"Finn, we have to get out of here," she said quickly. Her voice was tense, but she seemed to be working to keep her tone level. "You're bleeding really badly. Dad is going to have to patch you up really soon, but we can't stay here now. Something is going on in the city and father seems to think that we aren't safe anymore."

Eva began trying to lift me, but the moment she pulled under my arms, I screamed in pain and she quickly set me back down.

" I'm sorry Finn!" Eva gestured apologetically. "I'm going to need help to get you out of here, so just hang on and I'll find someone to help us. I don't know who's left in the house but I will find someone!"

She didn't wait for a response. She dashed off quickly into the darkness and again, I heard the door open and close.

"No, no....don't mind me. I'll just be right here. Bleeding out. No big deal." I said to the empty room. Sarcasm can be a wonderful tool in desperate circumstances.

While she was gone, I focused on breathing and trying to stay calm. I knew that if I allowed myself to have a complete meltdown that it would be ten times harder for her or anyone to actually help me. So I just focused on the silence and forced myself to breathe deeply. To my surprise, it actually seemed to be working. I slowly calmed down and the pain lessed just a bit.

A few minutes later, I heard the door open once again. I looked up and squinted into the darkness to see Eva rushing back to me with a young man on her heels. He was pushing a wheelchair of sorts, though it had a high back to it.

"Finn, this is Harris Archer. He was one of the guys who helped save you from falling."

"Charmed." I offered, through clenched teeth. He nodded at me and resumed setting up the wheelchair.

Eva gently grabbed hold of my left arm and Harris followed suit with my other arm.

She looked me square in the eyes and spoke quickly, "Alright, we're going to have to lift you up onto the chair and then we are going to get out of here. It is going to hurt a *lot*."

Oh *super*. Just what I wanted.

I must've made some sort of face because she shifted an inch or two closer to get a better grip and by the look she gave, it was clear she thought this was the only solution.

She continued, "If we don't get you out of here, I don't know what will happen to you. Everyone else has evacuated and it's just the three of us in the house at this point. My father had to leave for the council meeting a while ago, so we're going to take the Network and try and find some shelter for the time being."

I wasn't in a position to argue with her. Whereas I was a bit freaked out before with the whole "shaking house and scary explosion sounds followed by complete silence for what seemed like forever," her tone and the fact that everyone evacuated the house made me think twice about my personal safety.

Eva nodded to Harris, pulled up on the gag for me and gave me a moment to settle it between my teeth. On the count of three they lifted me into the chair. My face and arms were stuck to the ground from the blood already drying beneath me and it stung as they lifted me. I bit down hard on the pillow cover and tried not to scream wildly. In the longest second of my life thus far, they were able to situate me into the chair and before I knew it, we were rushing toward the door.

I felt light-headed and thirsty, but I shoved those thoughts away given the urgency to get out of the house seemed a bit more pressing at this point. Gently, I lowered the gag from my mouth using my good arm and attempt to help navigate. The dim glow coming from Eva's light was mildly helpful, as shapes and figures in the darkness gradually came into focus. The halls were lined with massive statues or suits of armor or metal casts of body parts that I assumed Giles used in his work.

I tried not to think too much about the decor (though my curious side was teeming with questions), but instead focused on the task at hand. We needed to get out of the house.

We rushed down the hallway, Eva leading the way. Harris was pushing my wheelchair quickly and trying to avoid any of the obstacles that had fallen down during the earthquake. Soon, we rounded a corner and were stopped by debris littering the hallway. Art, machines and tables were all overturned, scattered and broken throughout the hallway.

" Cogspit!" Harris blurted, his voice deep and rumbling. "There's no way I'm getting him over all of that in this chair."

"We will just have to find another way around then," Eva replied, coarsely.

We turned around to head back the other way and I noticed out of the corner of my eye something in the window where we had rounded the corner.

"Hey guys..." I said, lifting my arm to point toward the window. "I'm not from around here, but typically folks freak out when something tall and black with glowing blue eyes is staring in the window."

Their heads snapped to look at the window and something I can only assume was a curse left Eva's mouth and they both took off running, Harris pushing me and Eva darting through the debris on the ground.

"We can take the service lift to the subterrain from the back of the kitchen if we're quick," Eva called out over her shoulder to us.

Harris grunted an approval and continued pushing. I tried to help push the wheels with my hands, but I couldn't keep up with how quickly they were turning without wincing in pain and instead found myself slowing us down. Harris batted at my arm and ran on with renewed speed.

"I've got this Finn," he said between breaths. I nodded and pulled my hands into my lap and continued to stay on the lookout. I turned my head to look back at the figure in the window, but thankfully it was gone.

I breathed a sigh of relief and called out, "That thing is gone!"

Just then, the window next to Eva exploded inward with a shower of glass and a humongous black creature burst into the hallway. Its eyes burned bright blue in the darkness and its wings unfurled like a bat, stretching across the wide hallway. Eva screamed and was shoved aside in the blast. The light flew from her hand, skittered across the floor and went out and darkness flooded the hallway. Without hesitation, Eva righted her steps and didn't stop running. The creature flew down the hallway and grabbed at her with one of its long, sinewed arms. She ducked and pivoted down a corridor to her right just as the creature reached out. In its trail, tendrils of darkness followed it. Somehow, it seemed even darker than the house.

Harris turned the chair to follow Eva, throwing out one hand to slam the door behind us as we entered the new hallway.

"How big is your house?!" I called out to Eva.

"Right now, too big!" she called back over her shoulder, panting through breaths.

We heard a bang on the door behind us, but the solid metal and oak held firm against the creature.

Eva continued to weave through debris and other obstacles as Harris navigated the wheelchair like he had been doing this his whole life, no problem. We shot through two more rooms and then a third where we ended up in a smaller kitchen with a workstation in the middle.

"There!" Eva called out and pointed to a smaller door in the back corner of the room, near a pantry.

The pair dashed to the door and she yanked on the handle. It opened effortlessly and Harris pushed me into a freight elevator. Eva and Harris piled in behind my chair and pulled the metal gate down behind us, then mashed the button marked with an illuminated arrow pointing downward.

As the elevator lurched into motion, there was a loud thud and a screech that echoed through the kitchen. Before we were fully in motion, the creature flew into the kitchen and locked eyes with us. It barreled towards the lift door and yanked on the handle.

"That won't hold it for long," Harris said through labored breaths.

"It'll have to," Eva replied, bending over her knees, as she tried to slow her own breathing.

The lift slowly descended into increasing darkness until I couldn't even see my hand inches in front of my face.

No one spoke. I could tell they were exhausted and the adrenaline made me forget some of the searing pain from earlier. Now that we had a moment of rest, the pain flooded back and with it, a wave of nausea and lightheadedness.

I gripped the arms of the chair to keep from passing out and steadied myself against the methodical rattling of the elevator.

"Finn, are you okay?" Eva asked in the darkness.

"No, to be honest. But that's fine. Thanks for coming back for me," I said, eyes closed and just trying to focus on staying conscious. Blood seeped down over the chair edge from my arm and I *think* somewhere on my back.

"Yeah. No problem," she said, a hint of sarcasm in her voice combined with a nervous laugh.

A few more moments passed. The only sound in the darkness was the hum of the elevator, aside from the labored breathing from Eva and

Harris.

"What was that *thing*?" I asked finally.

"Voidkin," Harris replied, his deep voice blunt and echoing in the metal chamber.

I didn't know what that meant either, but I locked it away for another time. Harris' tone indicated no one was in a position to explain and now did not seem like the time for a history lesson.

"So, uhh, where are we headed?" I asked Eva, shifting gears.

"This lift will get us to the Network - a series of tunnels and passageways built by the Founders to help navigate the city in the event that the streets above became unsafe. We should be able to make our way to the Dragon's Barrow and from there, we should be able to contact my dad. He'll know what's going on by that point."

As she finished, the lift came to a halt and I heard Eva pull up on the grate. She opened the door to the tunnel and all three of us made that weird "hsssk!" sound through our teeth as light flooded into lift, momentarily blinding us. A few beats passed before my eyes adjusted and I saw small Edison bulbs lining a metal tunnel. The tunnel itself was probably five feet wide and maybe eight feet tall. Once we left the lift, Harris turned around, closed the gate, shut the metal door behind us and then grabbed a small piece of pipe laying on the ground and wedged it in the handle to stop the Voidkin from following us.

'I don't think that thing will be able to get to us now," Harris said quietly, more to himself than to anyone in particular.

We moved briskly down the corridor, though no one was running anymore. After probably a hundred yards or so, it branched off and we took the left passage. We snaked our way through corridors for probably 15 minutes. Periodically there appeared a door with a design etched into the center which seemed to give Eva and Harris an idea of where we were. Each time we opened a door, we took the time to close it behind us. Honestly, I would've been lost down there. With the doors shut behind us, there was little evidence that we had passed in that direction. During our trek, neither Eva or Harris spoke, instead focusing solely on the task at hand. After perhaps half an hour of brisk walking, we came to a door marked by a symbol of a dragon encircled by a cog.

Eva turned to us and smiled, "We made it. This is the door leading to the entrance of the

Dragon's Barrow. Once we're inside, let me do the talking. My father is friends with the owner, Kal, but most of the people who frequent the Dragon's Barrow are of... a less savory sort." She tried to be tactful, but I got the picture - guys who chose drinking in the underbelly of society usually weren't your typical law-abiding sort.

Eva continued, "I only met Kal once and I was much younger. I don't know what to expect in there, but chances are good if things are crazy up in the streets, this place will be even crazier. It's one of the only Barrows still in operation and it's possible that other people had the same idea we did. If nothing else, Ms. Weatherby should be here, along with a few of the other staff."

Harris nodded his assent and I gestured pulling a zipper over my lips. Eva turned the knob and pushed open the door.

Immediately, a din of voices flooded the hallway ahead of us. The tunnels we had worked our way through continued forward, but along the lefthand wall, a nook was etched out and brighter light spilled into the dim tunnel. Harris shut the door behind us and we marched toward the opening. A small metal plaque was affixed to the wall next to the nook with the same symbol that had been on the corridor door moments ago. We turned the corner, Eva took a deep breath to steel herself and we entered the Barrow.

CHAPTER TEN

Activity was everywhere. The Barrow looked to be something like a speakeasy - an underground tavern of sorts - dimly lit with a long bar along the back and tables and booths scattered throughout, all designed to be inconspicuous and unobtrusive to the naked eye. The door stood open and looked to be the same material of the tunnel walls behind us. If the door was shut, I imagine you'd have a hard time finding the Barrow.

The room busted with families, groups, cliques and the like. There was hardly any space to move around, and by the looks on their faces, they were scared. With the sheer number of people packed in there, you'd have thought it would be a lot louder. Instead, people whispered and huddled together. Some had gotten there early enough to snag a booth to sit down. Others were simply standing with their arms around their families, trying to comfort their children. Others yet were coping through intoxication. One man in particular, as we entered, fell off his stool and lay in a puddle of his own tears and drink. All of them were wearing the same type of clothes I'd seen Gladys and Eva wearing earlier, a strange mixture of civil-war era design mixed with utilitarian, yet fashionable updates. Some were wearing tall boots with the flaps turned down, comfortable yet classy pants, loose-fitting shirts and blouses, drawn together with either vests or overcoats with large brass buttons. Others were wearing functionally long dresses with various designs and small hats or full-blown evening gowns and tuxedos. Nothing looked quite right though, and if I had to sum it up for you, I'd venture to say I'd fallen into some kind of steampunk theme park and this was where the staff hung out.

Eva pushed through the crowd and headed for the back wall to the bar where a very frazzled looking older man hastily cleaned up a spilled drink on the oak bar top. Harris pushed me through as best he could, but we moved slowly and people, though accommodating my situation, were simply unable to move out of the way. The thought passed through my mind that if the terrifying creature that had found us at Eva's home got down here and into this room, the chaos alone would be devastating. It took us a while to get across the Barrow to where Eva, speaking with the man behind the bar.

"...So you see, he's bleeding and we need to get him some help quickly or it won't be long before he loses too much blood. I'm concerned it's already too late!" she said, nervously looking back and forth between the barkeep and me. I tried to look optimistic, but every few breaths, pain shot through my body like an electric pulse and I don't think I was hiding it well.

The man leaned in and spoke quietly to Eva. "Yeah, I see that. But we just don't have the space! We're maxed out down here. I don't know why everyone thought to come here, but I certainly don't have enough space or supplies to keep everyone down here for long," he said quietly to Eva, very obviously stressed. There were bags under his eyes and his voice, somewhat Cockney in nature, sounded frazzled.

"Look, Kal, can we just take him in your

freezer and try to redress his wounds? Then we will be out of your way, the chair won't be taking up any more room and we can help him out long enough to contact my dad and get him down here to help," Eva said, taking the bartender's hands in hers and doing her best to get me help. I've got to admit it, she is very charming when she wants to be.

Kal sighed heavily and rubbed a hand across his unshaven face and then shook his head in frustration. Clearly, this was not the night he planned on having.

"Yeah fine," he said, relenting to Eva. "But do not get blood everywhere. I get it, it's gonna be messy, but just try not to get it on everything back there, okay? It'll take me months to clean it and the stench will drive away my customers."

Eva squeezed his hands gently and leaned over to give him a kiss on the cheek. A smile touched the barkeep's lips and he then pulled away to tend another mess across the room.

Eva jerked her head toward the door in the back as inconspicuously as possible and Harris quickly wheeled me through it. The back room was as plain as the rest of the bar had been. A few metal crates lined the shelves,filled with various fixings that a bar might need - bottles of liquor, snacks and dishes. To the right, a large, thick metal door was latched shut. Eva pulled on the handle and yanked the door open. A blast of cool air spilled out of the room and Harris wheeled me into the walk-in freezer. Food stores and glassware lined the shelves on all sides of the room. Clearly, Kal was very organized and I'd bet tonight was giving him a bit of an anxiety attack. There wasn't a spot in the back rooms which was out of place or even remotely dirty.

Once in the freezer, Harris left for a few moments and I heard him in the other room gathering up a few things. A moment later, he walked back in and stepped around the front of my wheelchair. This was the first time I'd seen him in the light and I was surprised at his appearance. I'd heard him speak, albeit very briefly earlier in the tunnels and at the house. His voice was deep and rich and had a tone of confidence and authority about it. The man standing in front of me, though, looked more like an overgrown boy. Now I'm not one to talk, considering I'm mostly just arms and legs myself, but Harris just seemed too young for the voice I'd been hearing all night. His sandy blonde hair was cut short, but it was still long enough that the front had a slight curl to it and it framed his face nicely. His face was slightly round, but not chubby in any sense. His skin was incredibly smooth and he had a small birthmark or mole or something to the right of his mouth. All of this was stuffed into a body which was probably no more than 5'9" and was nothing but muscle all the way down. If I had to guess, I'd say his arms were probably the width of my torso.

He leaned down, gently took hold of my wrist and looked me in the eyes.

"I'm sorry again, but I'm going to have to pick you up and lay you down. The cold floor will help slow your bleeding and I need to change your bandages. Eva went to call her dad and see if he can get down here to help out. He's really the only one at this point who we know that will be able to fix your injuries," he said, his deep voice surprisingly relaxed.

I nodded once and closed my eyes to prepare for the inevitable shocks of pain. I felt his arms wrap gently around my torso and he lifted me from the chair. A wave of burning hot pain ripped through my stomach, back and legs and I drew in a sharp breath. In one smooth motion, Harris took me from sitting to standing to lying on the ground.

He placed me face down on the ground and stripped off my robe and then began undoing the bandages on my back. With every movement he made, new waves of agony crashed through my body. Soon, however, he removed the tape and gauze, the layers of bandages and then, finally, the shell which was holding it all in place.

I tried to turn to look as best as I was able, but I couldn't see my back very well.

"Hey, any chance they have a mirror in here somewhere? I haven't seen it yet and I'm kind of curious," I asked Harris.

"Doubt it," he said, briefly looking around the freezer. "I'm not sure Kal is in need of a mirror while he catalogs his food stores."

"Fair enough," I replied through clenched teeth, trying to forget the horrible pain.

"Honestly, I don't think it is that bad, considering what you looked like before we got you to Dr. Flemming," Harris continued. "Your body looked like it had been through a meat grinder at that point. Your skin had split open in a bunch of spots and your bones were poking through the skin in a few as well. We were all thinking it was too late and you'd never really recover, that is, if you regained consciousness at all." As he spoke, he tore several strips off a tablecloth from the storeroom.

"Actually, considering it has only been a few weeks, you've made remarkable progress. I've helped Dr. Flemming a few times with patients and I've been involved with a number of their physical therapy sessions, as well as redressing their wounds and none of them have looked this good this soon," he said as he finished tearing the tablecloth and began pressing strips to my back. I winced, but it didn't hurt as much as it had a few moments before.

"Well, that's something, at least," I replied. "Oh, and I didn't get to thank you for saving me either. Eva said it was you and a few other guys who managed to break my fall."

"Yeah, Trent and Lucky were there and we were working on Trent's Caster when Eva shouted at us about some guy falling through the sky. We looked up, and there you were, tumbling head over heels in the open air. A moment later, a Curator smashed into you and fortunately, it actually flung you a lot closer to our direction. So, Trent and I grabbed his globe and ran over to you. Lucky was already climbing the lattices to get closer to you and we tossed it up to him. Man, he lives up to his name because just as he caught it he activated it and tossed it under you just in time."

"Globe?" I asked while I attempted to hold my breath, trying in part to just continue to the conversation so I'd be distracted from the excruciating pain. Also, because I was curious.

"Yeah, you know. His photon globe," he said, matter of fact.

"Oh, of course. *That* globe. Naturally. How could I have forgotten?"

He pushed a little bit more on the bandage he was applying and I drew in another sharp breath.

"You've got a mouth on you, don't you?" he said, pulling a roll of what looked like packing tape out from behind him.

"For good or bad. Mostly bad, I suppose," I said, awkwardly lifting my hands behind me in a placating gesture.

"Yeah, well, Eva told me about your conversation from earlier. I don't know what happened with you but if she believes that you aren't from here, then I'm inclined to agree." He tore off a piece of clear tape and pressed it to my back.

"A photon globe is a small device we use to hold objects in stasis when we're working. When you turn it on, it projects a small field of electromagnetic energy. You can manipulate the energy field to different shapes and sizes depending on the kind of task you need it for. Typically people have a few around the house for the odd task, but it's mostly used by mechanics. They'll toss a few cogs, screws, and gears in there and it makes it easier to grab hold of them with greasy hands."

"Sounds really useful," I chimed in.

"It is, and in your case, life changing." He tore off another piece of tape and pressed it onto my back to hold the bandages.

"It isn't designed to do much more than hold a few pounds. But, when Lucky tossed it, it projected a field underneath you which caused your body to slow enough that when you hit the ground, it was more like you'd jumped from a few stories instead of several hundred. It was still a hard hit on the ground, but it was way better than it could've been."

He finished adhering the tape to the bandage and examined his handiwork. I could feel his cool hands against my back as he gently pressed to see if there were any other places he missed.

"Alright. I think that's it," Harris said with a

tone of completion. "We're going to have to turn you on your back to let the cold ground do its work to reduce the swelling and get the bleeding to slow."

Before I could reply, he placed one hand gently on my back between the shoulder blades and the other on my shoulder and pulled me over. My chest was red from the cold and I could see the bruising that wrapped around my sides from my back. Harris started in on my arm next, since the bandages covering that were also completely undone. My left arm was black and blue and purple from shoulder to wrist, save for the stitches. The scabs and stitching looked like a lightning bolt struck me and etched a trail through the veins in my arm.

Quietly, Harris worked to redress the gauze on my arm and within a few minutes everything was done. He helped me into my robe once more and I tried to lie calmly on the cold ground and allow the freezer to help numb the pain away.

"Thanks," I offered quietly, my eyes shut as I lay there.

"Yeah," he said, grabbing up the used bandages and balling them into a pile to toss into the trash bin. Even in these few short interactions, it struck me that Harris was a man of few words. What words he spent in a conversation usually carried weight.

Just then, Eva walked back into the freezer. "Oh good, you're all done. How's he doing?" she asked Harris.

"His bleeding is slowed and the tablecloth should work for a while. He's going to need more help than I can get him right now though," Harris replied as if he was simply giving a medical history.

"Well, that's good then. I just spoke to my dad and I don't think he's going to be able to come any time soon." Her face was sullen and exhausted. Little circles were starting to darken underneath her eyes and she didn't have the same energy she had a few minutes earlier.

"Why? What's going on?" Harris asked, his deep voice curt as he tossed the pile of garbage into the bin.

Eva looked around cautiously and closed the door from the Barrow to the back room and then leaned in to whisper.

"Something is happening. Somehow the Void has gotten free and at least one of the 12 hasn't been heard from. The others are still piecing things together and dad isn't sure what any of this means."

Harris stopped abruptly and his eyes grew wide.

"How?"

That one word from deep in his chest carried an immense amount of weight behind it.

Eva shrugged, her expression tired and seemingly out of answers. Harris visibly shivered and then resumed cleaning up the storeroom. Eva walked over to me and leaned over to check my bandages.

Watching this whole exchange, I felt a little bit out of place. I raised my left hand, fingers extended, in a 'teacher will you call on me' gesture and cleared my throat.

"Hey, uh, guys. I know I'm just the new kid on the block but..." I looked from one to the other, "whats the Void?"

A gentleman's voice with a strong Cockney accent chimed in from the door to the tavern behind Eva and Harris, "It is singularly the darkness that consumes."

CHAPTER ELEVEN

All three of us turned to look and saw Kal, the bartender, carrying three bowls filled with something that smelled delicious. He motioned to Harris to take a bowl from his hand, as he balanced a third bowl on his forearm.

"The Void is the death that comes for us all and only by the Ember do we still live."

Ok. Well, so that wasn't exactly the kind of response I was hoping for. I guess with a title like "the Void" it's not likely to be pleasant. Still, Kal's doom-and-gloom outlook seemed a bit heavy handed.

Eva took her bowl and the other from Kal and set it down next to me. She leaned over and offered to help me eat if I needed, gesturing with the spoon in her hand. I shook my head and sat up a little, wincing each time I moved. I was able to gently lean against a nearby shelf, and thankfully, I think the cold was working because everything hurt a lot less. With my good arm, I grabbed the bowl of soup and set it on my lap.

I chimed in, taking a spoonful of warm soup to my lips before asking, "I'm sorry, I just don't get it. What is it and how did it get here?"

Kal's eyes narrowed and it seemed as though he was trying to discern something very important. A moment passed and then his features softened. He put up a finger in a gesture of "wait a second" and walked back to the bar. He returned with a wooden stool and a bowl of soup for himself.

"Aye, well, it seems as though we're going to be in here a long while," Kal said, sitting and gesturing with his head toward the bar room. "The place is packed and people are scared. I don't see anyone leaving until the 12 get their act together or the Arcmagus does something dramatic. I'd rather be back here with you lot than out there with a hoard of crying children and mothers who I can't do anything for." He took a large spoonful of soup and then licked his lips. He made satisfied sound and he nodded his approval to himself.

"So what is the Void, huh?" he said, reflectively, his accent thick as he chewed over the words. "Don't get outside much, do you lad?"

I stared at him, unsure how to respond.

"He's been, uhh, sick. The fall he took really messed up his head," Eva offered in my defense.

"That I can see," Kal said, leaning forward, looking me up and down. "Well, the Void is what remains of the time of the Culling. It is a real, visible presence outside our city which threatens at any moment to overrun us," he said, leaning back on his stool and folding his arms over his chest. "Or at least *used* to threaten. It appears that something has changed all that. The reports I got from the first few folks rushing in here, it seems the Void swept over the whole city and is just holding. No Voidkin or anything have been seen, but it's just a matter of time."

The three of us looked at one another with knowing glances. Harris went back to eating his soup and Eva started playing with her hair. Kal never took his eyes off of me but it was clear he got the picture. He sighed once heavily and rubbed a hand over his face.

"Well, let us hope that the 12 actually *can* do

something about it. We should be alright down here as long as the Ember holds, but this place wasn't meant to be a refuge. I only have a few meals worth of food and certainly not for everyone out there."

Just then, a loud click sounded like the one I heard in the house earlier when the darkness came and that same voice chimed on the intercom.

"Citizens of Emberwall. A red alert curfew is now in effect. Do not proceed outside under any circumstances. Secure shelter and await instruction. The Proterezar is in session. The Arcmagus will protect us." And then there was silence, a click, and the message then repeated.

"Great," Kal said, sighing and tossing a hand in the air in frustration.

We sat there, looking at one another, silence hanging in the air after the message. Then, a loud crash tore through the other room, and that's when the screaming started.

CHAPTER TWELVE

Eva stood with a jolt. Harris stopped eating mid bite. Kal and I looked at each other wide eyed. All told, I think our reflexes were pretty impressive.

Kal bounded to his feet and threw open the door from the storeroom to the bar area. Screams flooded the room, punctuated by the sound of breaking furniture or horrible tearing sounds and then abrupt silence. Kal looked over his shoulder at us and hissed, "Voidkin!"

He shut the door and barred it quickly, then rushed to Eva and fumbled for something in his pockets.

"Here, take these keys. They'll unlock the supply freighter out back. It'll take you to the central hub of the Network and get you close to Emberhollow. I know your father has a plan, but we are in no position to take on an army of Voidkin. Send word to him that they've reached the Network and we must act quickly. I'm going to try and save as many as I can and we'll hop on the next freighter."

He shoved a bundle of keys into Eva's hands and without waiting for a response, he turned on his heel, and grabbed a pole from the storeroom wall. In one fluid motion, he hit a small dragon symbol on the far wall of the storeroom and the wall itself slid open, revealing another tunnel. In the same motion, he flung open the door to the bar and turned the latch so it would lock behind him. People were still screaming and the sounds of fighting poured in once more.

"Cogspit!" Harris said, dropping his bowl and getting to his feet. "I'm going after him. He can't..."

Eva interrupted, "No, Archer. I need you. More importantly, Finn needs you. I can't get him around as quickly as you and we don't have time to waste. We need to get to my dad and find out how to stop this."

His hands balled into fists and I saw Harris

flex them noticeably with frustration.

"Fine. Let's get going. The sooner this is over, the better," he said, bending back down to me, grabbing hold of my good arm. He looked me in the eye and I nodded once to him. Together, we managed to get me back into the chair with a lot less pain than before and pushed me toward the hallway.

We hurried down the long corridor, Eva rushing ahead of us. At the end there was a cart that looked like a trolley car. It was wooden, except for the frame, which was crafted of one solid piece of silver metal. The design on the side of the car intermixed ornate metals of gold, bronze and silver along with pieces of machinery that looked more decorative than functional. There were cogs, sprockets, prongs, gears and all manner of oddities. Instead of being on tracks like a normal trolley, though, the cart was suspended in the air by a single rail above where it swayed slightly.

Timed perfectly, Harris got me into the car just as Eva got the key into the lock and flung open the door. It opened like a minivan cabin door, sliding off to the side as Eva pulled on it. We hustled into the freighter and Harris rolled me to a side and snagged the keys from Eva. No conversation passed between the two, instead they seemed to simply know what to do. Harris jammed the key into the ignition, pushed several buttons, and then pulled on a large lever which extended from the floor up to the conductor's chair. A flash of blue light pulsed on the outside of the trolley along the entire frame and track which held the car suspended in air.

Just then, a crash sounded down the tunnel toward the Barrow and I looked up to see the door from the bar room burst inward. A torrent of dark smoke poured out of the bar.

"Guys..." I called out, gripping the arms of the wheelchair in anticipation, "we've got to go!"

I saw the glowing blue eyes of the Voidkin moving quickly down the hall. Harris was working the control panel and Eva was trying to secure the door of the trolley.

"Guys!" I called out again, my heartbeat racing in my chest.

Eva's head snapped toward Harris and she nodded once.

"Punch it," She said with an eerie calmness.

Harris flipped a lever and the trolley took off. The force of the acceleration pulled my wheelchair backward until I was pressed against the back wall of the tram, opposite the conductor's room. It was pitch black in the tunnels ahead of us, save for the glowing blue track of the trolley which seemed to illuminate only moments ahead of us. As we shot through the dark, our speed continued to increase, the velocity made my head swim and my vision blurred. Darkness edged into my sight and a strange sensation came over me.

It's daytime. I'm hovering over a city, but falling head over heels toward my death. The city is huge and a massive metal wall stands like a monolith hedging in the buildings, pulsating with an eerie red-orange glow. The wall seemed to stretch off in one direction well beyond what I can see. In the other direction, the structure dead ends in a massive mountain which looks like a volcano, pulsating with that same glow. Beyond the wall and all around the city is darkness, but above is a glorious blue sky with the sun shining. It seems like only the city is illuminated and the rest of the world covered in darkness. A few towers rise high above the rest but I can't even see the entire city. As the wind rushes around me, it strikes me that the city must be the size of a country. Just then, I see something coming toward me, fast. It looks like a robot. That can't be right...It isn't slowing down. It's going to hit me. No. Please. Wait. I just want to go home. I throw out my arms in front of me trying vainly to stop it. The machine slams into my left side and pain shoots through my arm and torso. I black out.

Pain shot through my arm and torso and I drew in a sharp breath. My vision went back to normal and my head cleared. From across the car Eva looked at me, holding on to one of the poles that lined every few feet of the freighter.

"Is everything okay?" she asked as concern creased her forehead. Her voice was calm and surprisingly reassuring. Something about that barely noticeable accent really calmed me down.

I shifted slightly in the wheelchair and tried to get more comfortable.

"Yeah. Thanks," I replied, waving a hand in a 'yeah, I'm totally fine, but not really' gesture.

She seemed to digest that for a moment before she nodded, walked down the cabin toward me and sat on a bench near me. We sat in silence for a few moments as the tram blazed a trail in the dark tunnel.

A bit unsure what to do, I cleared my throat and looked at Eva.

"Hey, so I've been meaning to ask," I said, placing my hands in my lap and looked out the window behind us. Yeah, its nearly pitch black out there, save for the glow from the rail. So what? Guys don't like to talk and it makes it easier if we don't have to look at the other person while we do it. It's why we like campfires and video games. We can have a good conversation, but we have something else to look at so it doesn't get all awkward.

I continued, "Why...uh," I cleared my throat again, finding my mouth surprisingly dry. "Why did you come back for me? And, perhaps more to a point, why have you and Harris taken care of me?" I couldn't bring myself to look directly at her, so I continued staring out the window, occasionally looking down at my lap.

"What do you mean?" Eva said coolly. "Why *wouldn't* I?"

The emphasis she put on her reply made me flinch slightly.

"No, no, I'm really grateful," I said, turning to look at her and putting my hands out in a placating manner. "But, I mean, you don't even know me. We've had one real conversation and the rest of the time, I've been unconscious or basically screaming in pain. But when all the craziness started going down, you came for me and even brought Harris to help me."

Eva shrugged and this time it was her turn to avoid eye contact. She fidgeted for a moment and then started playing mindlessly with her hair. "It's the right thing to do, I guess. It's not like you could've gotten out of the house on your own. And even though I didn't know there would be Voidkin, it seemed cruel to leave you in the house in the dark to fend for yourself when you couldn't even get out of bed without tearing open your back."

"True enough." I said, letting the thought hang in the air for a moment.

"Plus," she added, sweeping her hair out of her face with a hand, "I told you I believed you. I promised to help you figure out what was going on and I can't very well help with that if you're lying in a puddle of your own blood on the floor of my guest room while the entire world is headed for the Cogs. I don't know if you've caught on but this sort of thing," she gestured outside aimlessly, "doesn't happen every day around here."

"Well, thanks." I smiled at her and then quickly shifted my gaze back out the window.

I cleared my throat again and changed topics. "So, what do you think happened to all those people in the bar?"

Her face darkened a bit and her smile faded. "I don't really want to think about it. They're probably all dead at this point. There really isn't a way any of them made it out of there unless Kal..." She stopped mid sentence and closed her eyes. Her voice was shaky and she took a moment to steady herself.

I reached out best I could and rested my hand on her forearm. She put her other hand on mine and I gently squeezed her arm to reassure her.

"Sorry I brought it up," I said apologetically.

"No..." she started but her voice caught and it took her a moment. "No, it's okay. I've known Kal most of my life and while I haven't seen him much of late, it hurts to think that he may have died trying to protect us."

I nodded and silence settled in as I gave her space to grieve. The trolley shot through the darkness and the sound of the mechanisms clicking and changing was oddly soothing. I looked around and tried to come up with something else to talk about to get her mind off what just happened.

"So, how did Harris know how to operate this thing? And where are we going?"

Eva took another moment to finish composing herself and wiped a tear from the corner of her eye. She looked up and took in a breath, then glanced over at Harris who was stalwartly looking out the front entryway with one hand placed firmly on the conductor's console.

"He doesn't," she replied honestly as she cleared her throat. "But thankfully there is only one track, and Kal gave us the key, so I imagine he just pushed buttons until everything turned on."

"Oh, I guess that makes sense," I said. "Where does this take us?"

"I'm not exactly sure," she replied, shrugging her shoulders. "But all of the freight lines head to a central hub over in Emberhollow, the first Ward. Since we're trying to get to my dad in the council chambers, that's where we need to go. From there, it'll just be a matter of getting to some of the upper levels within the ward itself."

"All right then," I replied, adjusting my robe

as I noticed it had slipped awkwardly off my shoulder. "Hopefully he'll be able to make sure I didn't completely rip something open, or do irreparable damage to my back. That said, I've been feeling a lot better over the course of the last hour or so. Ever since we got to the Barrow and I got to lie on the cool floor, everything has been feeling a whole lot better!"

"Oh I am so glad!" she said, mustering a smile. "I was worried when we found you in the guest quarters on the floor. It looked like you had lost a lot of blood! I know that the last few weeks have been really rough on you but I'm glad you are feeling better. "

Yes, *really rough* might be an understatement, especially considering I can't remember any of those "few weeks" aside from nearly dying and waking up in excruciating pain and all of the events of this hellish evening.

I smiled back, unsure how to continue the conversation and went back to staring out the window. It must just be a habit of mine at this point with all of the driving around from job to job over the last few years. I like to look out the window and enjoy the scenery, daydreaming about what things could be like. I always enjoyed looking at the mountains in Tucson, just wondering what's going on out there. Wondering what kind of wildlife was busy making a home, or what kind of predators were stalking their prey, or what kind of insects were crawling all about trying to just survive. It always fascinated me that there are entire ecosystems of life that exist well beyond my perception. They continue on with life as though there is nothing more important in the world than finding that next berry or building a nest or protecting the queen.

Yet for me, most of my life I've spent trying to figure out what's next. Dead end jobs and unrewarding schooling and all the other areas of life I've explored up to now just seemed rather trivial. But the little ground squirrel scurrying around the desert, making sure there was food for the evening while not being food for something else - that was a life I found I envied. The squirrel knew what to do and how to enjoy the moment and there were no question marks about where to go from there. Even now, when I've been broken into little pieces and being pushed around by strangers in an odd world with a terrifying demon somewhere behind us, I still don't know where to go next. I don't even know how to get home.

I find staring out the window helps calm me and helps me to focus. As I stared out the window now, I was greeted with only darkness. I didn't know if we were still in a tunnel, or if we had gotten somewhere outside, all was still pitch black.

"You know…" I started to say, but stopped mid-sentence as I spotted something in the darkness behind us. I could see the faint outline of something glowing far behind us. The glow was slowly but definitely gaining on our position. I squinted to see it better, and realized it was the eyes of the horrifying creature that had been chasing us.

My head snapped to face the front of the cabin and I yelled, "Harris! That thing is gaining on us! It's a ways off, but I can see its eyes behind us and it's definitely going to catch up!"

Without hesitation, Harris threw a lever coming from the floor as far forward as it would go. The freighter picked up speed and I was pushed back against the wall once again. We were already going at intense speeds, but now we were shooting through the darkness with nauseating intensity, to the point that the cabin began shaking as our speed increased.

The sudden shaking jostled Eva against the side of her bench, and it took her a moment to recover. Briefly we locked eyes and I noticed concern etched on her face. She shook it off and turned to stare steel-eyed out the back window.

The glowing eyes were growing ever larger as the beast gained on us. Harris worked fiercely at the control panel, trying to get us moving quicker, but the car wasn't fast enough to stay ahead of the creature. I called out to Harris update him as he worked the controls. Eva stood and pulled her way forward through the cabin intent on helping Harris.

Still gaining speed, the entire car began to shake violently. I'm sure that these things were never designed to be in a high speed chase versus a nightmare beast, and it was clear we were losing. Eva worked her way to the helm pulling against the force of our forward motion and had to stop every other step to hold onto something to not lose her balance. I could see she was struggling and it was frustrating that I wasn't able to help. All I could do was let Harris know how close the Voidkin was to our position. I hated being in this chair. I felt so useless and pathetic and I hated every minute of it.

As I sat stewing over my predicament, we must have emerged from the tunnel. Just before Eva reached the cabin with Harris, a second Voidkin came out of nowhere and smashed broadside into our car.

The car faltered and swayed on the hinge that held us to the rail. Already shaking from the speed, the freighter made a sound like metal tearing and sparks flew down around the cabin, momentarily lighting up the darkness just beyond us. As the Voidkin hit the car, Eva was sent flying into the windows. Glass spewed out behind us and Eva landed on the floor with a thud. She didn't move.

Harris was also jolted from his post. I watched Eva slam into the wall, but Harris held his footing better. He was brought to a knee, but he held onto the console and that helped to steady him. He immediately pulled himself up and continued working at the gears. He took both hands and placed them directly on the empty space of the console. For a moment I worried that he was going to pass out or something, but then a sudden flash of blue sparks left his fingertips and burrowed into the console. Renewed, the trolley took on new speeds and everyone was pulled backwards once again. Stupid inertia.

I called out to Harris, "Eva's been hit and isn't moving!"

"Cogspit!" he snapped and then turned his

head to look at me. "I can't take my hands off of the console here or we're dead in the water. Can you get to her?"

"I'm sure gonna try!" I took hold of the wheels of my chair and pushed as hard as I could against the force of the trolley moving forward. I expected there to be more pain in my arm, but surprisingly it didn't hurt much, save for a dull ache. The trolley shot through the darkness and I pushed with all of my strength to get to Eva. Every few moments, the cabin shook so hard it jostled me against the seats. I made progress, but it was slow going.

Sometimes I forget how loud everything is when you're in motion. If you were in your car, going a few hundred miles an hour with the windows down and you have a flat tire or two and your engine is making a horrible noise, that would be deafening. This was significantly worse than that, now that the Voidkin hit us. Metal screeched as wheels clicked methodically along the rails. When Eva hit the window, it broke and the oppressive noise of rushing wind filled the cabin. Combined with the periodic shuddering of the entire freighter, it was insanely loud. To top it all off, I had no idea where the Voidkin was who hit the trolley. I glanced back to see if I could make out the features of the other creature. Sure enough, its eyes were glowing brightly several dozen yards back.

After what seemed like an eternity, I made it halfway down the cabin. Another loud screech of tearing metal ripped through the night and a new wave of sparks showered from the gears above and fell on the outside of the cabin. In the afterglow, I now saw two Voidkin keeping pace behind us by only a few yards. Trying to ignore them, I pushed myself forward to get to Eva's unconscious body. She must have hit the wall hard to still be out. I could feel the muscles in my left arm working hard to keep up with the strain, pushing against our momentum.

Finally, I managed to get close enough to her. I wedged my chair between a bench and a pole usually used, I assume, for standing passengers and took a deep breath. I bent over and reached for her arm. Pain pooled in my back and spread out over my entire midsection. Again, it wasn't the sharp stabbing pain I had experienced earlier, but it definitely hurt. I grimaced and wrapped my good hand around Eva's wrist and pulled with all my might. The force of the trolley helped a little and in a moment, her head and torso were slung over my lap. I heaved her to the side and managed to get most of her body onto the bench beside me. I grabbed her legs and swung those onto the bench as well. With her in place, I moved my chair beside her to act as a barrier so she wouldn't go flying off anywhere in the event something else happened.

"How much further? Can you tell?" I called out to Harris.

"No way to know for sure," he called back, never taking his eyes off the window in front of him. "We were coming from the far reaches and it's usually several hours to get to the Emberhollow. But usually that's with stops in all the other Wards along the way and any number of other delays."

"Well, crap." The words left my lips like poison. I shouted back, "I've got Eva here on a bench and I'm blocking her in. She doesn't look too bad from the outside considering the hit she took and she is definitely breathing, but otherwise she isn't moving." I wheeled my chair in front of her midsection to help block her into the seat in case the cabin shook.

"There's not much else we can do until we get to Central!" Harris yelled over the noise. Sparks periodically leapt from his hands to the console and the trolley pushed faster and faster with each passing moment.

"I don't know what you're doing, but the faster we get there, the better! Those things are still out there and we can't take another hit like that," I said, looking out the back window. The blue glow of the Voidkin still menacingly maintained an uncomfortable close distance.

"I'm doing everything I can!" Harris called out, as sweat beaded down his forehead and darkened his shirt.

"Just out of curiosity," I shouted while investigating Eva's head for any sign of bruising or swelling, "is it normal that there aren't any other trains on this rail? Seems to me like we should have seen a few by now."

"Good question. I don't really want to think about catching up to another freighter."

"Will you be able to stop us when we reach the station?" I asked.

"We'd better hope so! We're going way too fast for normal brakes. If I were to stop us now we'd snap right off the rail and plummet a couple hundred feet!" He squinted and it seemed to me like he was trying to see ahead, even though none of the light from the trolley made an impact on the impenetrable darkness.

I tried not to think about if we made it to the station or met up with another car on the tracks what might happen to us, so I busied myself with trying to see if Eva had really hit her head. I moved her red hair gently until I spotted a small bruise forming under the skin, right behind her right ear. It was only a little swollen, but I knew from experience that even a little swelling on the head can lead to some serious complications. I needed to relieve the pressure so it didn't cause any substantial damage.

"Harris, you got anything to help with swelling?"

"Nah, sorry!" He called back. "But Eva usually has something like that on her. She uses a multitool at work."

I searched her pockets and sure enough, clipped to the hem of her left front pocket was a small tool. I slid it from her pocket and tried to open it. When I heard "multitool" I assumed it was one of those combination pliers, screwdriver, knife tool thing that mechanics and the like keep on them. This was not that tool. Naturally. Why would anything in this place be normal?

Instead, this contraption was a solid piece of

metal about 4 inches long and 2 inches wide. It had a button on one end that when pressed, extended a prong out one end of the device. It looked a little like one of those pokey meat forks with just the two big prongs that's useful for getting meat on and off the grill. Between the two prongs, though, there was a beam of blue electricity. It reminded me a little bit of a taser or somesuch.

"Uhh, I don't think this'll work," I said, turning the multitool over in my hand.

"Then it'll have to wait!" Harris called. "I think we're coming up on the entrance to Central now! You'd better hang onto something. I don't know how fast we're going to stop!"

Before we started slowing, a third Voidkin came out of nowhere and slammed into the side of our cart. I had just enough time to grab ahold of one of the poles before I got tossed to the side. The force of the collision made a tremendous crashing sound - adding shattering windows, wood cracking and more metal tearing to an already overwhelmingly loud and tense situation. I was able to keep hold for a moment and in turn, keep Eva from flying off her seat. Harris was jolted from his post and went slamming into the wall next to him. He didn't hit the wall as hard as Eva had earlier and thankfully, got up quickly. As soon as his hands left the console, though, the train started slowing down so violently it began shook and twisted in the air.

Harris tried to regain his footing and put his hands back on the gears but it was too late. Every second that passed, more metal was sheared away from the cart. A moment later, there was a horrid snapping sound and the rail that held our trusty little car snapped in half and our car flew off the tracks at terrifying speed toward the abyss below.

CHAPTER THIRTEEN

I threw my body over top of Eva as best I was able and held tightly to the poles next to us. Unnerving quiet filled the train as it left the track and my stomach lurched as we settled into a free fall.

The freighter smashed into the ground and sent Harris flying again. I barely hung on and grabbed Eva to keep from falling off the bench. With a horrid screech, the tram sailed for several hundred feet along the floor, smashing into object after object I couldn't see but heard before finally slowing to a stop. Fortunately we didn't smash into anything large or we wouldn't have walked out of there alive.

I heard coughing from where Harris had

been and it took me a moment before I could move once the dust settled. Harris coughed again, spit up something and then stood to his feet. He was bleeding down one arm and his clothes were torn all over. I sat up and uncovered Eva, and looked down to see that she was okay and breathed a sigh of relief. Harris stumbled over, stabilizing himself against the wall.

"Are you alright?" I asked.

"Mmnn," he replied, nodding his head as he did so. He rubbed his face and shook his head, clearing the haze.

"We were close to the station. I think we landed just inside the station door. Otherwise we would've fallen a *lot* further and we'd all probably look more like you did several weeks ago."

"Just what I needed, another lesson on the reality of gravity," I said.

"Yeah, well, let's get Eva and see if we can get to the council. We need to get there pretty much yesterday."

I nodded and lifted Eva from the bench. She was limp but also small, so it wasn't much trouble for me, even with a busted arm and back.

Harris came over and scooped her up and held her cradled in his arms. He wasn't a tall man, but he was well built and Eva looked like a child in his arms.

"Can you take care of yourself?" he asked.

"I should be okay. As long as I can get out the door and onto the ground, I should be fine to wheel myself. I don't know what you did to me back in the Barrow, but I feel a hundred times better."

Harris grunted and set Eva down gently on a bench near the door. We spent a few moments navigating the wreckage to get me and the wheelchair out of the cabin and then he went back, grabbed Eva and we pressed on into the darkness.

By now, I was getting used to how dark it was. There had been dim light in the cabin of the trolley and in the Barrow but the darkness seemed to have settled on the entire city and it was almost as though nighttime never wanted to give up. The unsettling thing about the darkness, though, was that we couldn't see if something was coming for us. Three Voidkin had been chasing after us for some time and I couldn't imagine they were giving up just as our train derailed. Although, then again, I have no idea *why* they were chasing us. It seemed as though the people in the Barrow had gotten there just fine without anything chasing them. Did we accidentally lure that creature down to the depths and get those people killed? And what about the staff from Dr. Fleming's house? Ms. Weatherby wasn't in the Barrow when we got there, which hopefully meant she wasn't attacked like those poor people, but it also doesn't solve where she or any others would've gone. We seemed to have all the luck of a gambling addict hoping for another big score at the casino. All the right choices, all the wrong results. I just had so many questions and no answers for anything.

As I worked through these issues, Harris slowly led us through the darkened corridors of the train depot. What I could make out of the depot, it seemed pretty grandiose but very old. There were wooden benches spaced periodically and large pillars made of burnished metal. Given that we were stumbling around in the darkness, that's just about all I could make out.

The further into the station we got, the more something just felt completely off. I couldn't put my finger on it. Don't get me wrong, I was pleased that for the time being, the Voidkin weren't chasing us and we gradually were getting closer to our destination. Hopefully, Dr. Fleming would be able to fix me up and help his daughter too. Still, I couldn't shake the feeling that someone or some*thing* was out there waiting to nab us.

We entered a hallway with stairs leading up out of the train depot itself and made our way past the entry gate. Harris looked at me and my chair and then sighed heavily.

"There should be a lift somewhere which will get us upstairs to the landing bay. That should allow us to get to the thoroughfare and then to the lifts heading to the top levels of Central. The Proterezar chambers are in the penthouse of the Ward." Harris said. He shrugged his shoulders slightly and tilted his head, clearly getting sore from carrying Eva and the crash earlier. Blood still pulsed periodically from his arm, but he seemed to manage alright.

"I'll follow you," I replied, turning my chair and pushing myself behind him as he looked for the lift. We found it and made our way to the main level of the depot. There was an eerie stillness about the entire place. The darkness felt thicker up here than it did down in the tunnels and the hair on the back of my neck began to stand on edge.

"Harris, something feels off," I said quietly in the darkness.

"Yeah, I don't like it either," he replied,

gathering Eva closer to himself and moving a little bit quicker than he had a moment earlier.

"Do you know where to go?" I asked

"Most of the Wards are built similarly. They may have different layouts but they all generally build the vertical ascension the same. Once we get out of the train depot, we should be on the main road on this level and then the lifts should be about three blocks down the road. As long as there is still power, we should be ok. I just don't want to linger out in the open any longer than necessary. Hopefully the Voidkin got distracted with our crash and we can sneak through here."

"Well, I'm feeling okay, so if you want to hustle, I say we do it."

"Alright then, follow close and try not to get cut off," Harris replied.

He peered left and right, checking for Voidkin and then quickly marched out the large glass door entryway of the train depot.

I pushed my chair closely behind Harris trying to avoid accidentally tripping him and did my best to not get distracted. It was difficult though, considering the sheer size of the city. In the dark, I could see the outlines of massive buildings lining the road on either side. The road itself was wide and made of cobblestone, but looked more like a six lane boulevard back home. It was completely empty of all life though, and that made the size all the more daunting.

Harris walked as fast as he could without jostling Eva and I was pushed alongside him, keeping a wary eye out for any glowing blue eyes that might be following us. So far, thankfully, there were none.

We passed a side street that led into pitch darkness and continued forward. All along the boulevard, vacant storefronts and businesses reinforced my fear and I was barely able to hold it together as we pushed on. I opened my mouth to ask Harris how close we were when a dim light popped through the darkness and a door clicked open next to us.

"What're you kids doing out there!" an older woman hissed in our direction.

"We have to get to Central," Harris replied without looking over.

"It isn't safe out there! You need to get inside!" She called back through a hoarse whisper.

"Just shut the door, ma'am and stay inside," Harris calmly replied, his deep voice quiet but confident and never taking his eyes off course.

The woman scowled at us and then shut her door quietly and flicked off the lights again. We kept moving quickly through the street as quietly as possible.

A moment later, Harris leaned over to me and whispered, "There! The lift is just up ahead. Come on!"

He took off at a jog and I pushed to keep up with him. We made it to the elevator and pressed the button to call it. The door to the elevator had a beautiful intricate design that looked like that of an old elevator from the early 1900s. Brass and silver squares with impressions on them of geometric shapes lined the metal doors and a small light above the door showed that the lift was currently up on the 87th floor. It wasn't a fast-moving lift but it seemed that shouldn't take more than a few moments for it to come.

We put our backs to the wall continuing to watch behind us for any sort of movement or anything that might be coming towards us. I still had that sinking feeling that something was wrong but so far things were going alright, considering.

"Where do you suppose the Voidkin are?" I asked Harris, not taking my eyes off the darkness in front of us.

"I'm not sure, but I'm grateful they didn't follow us here," Harris replied.

Just then, Eva began to stir. She lifted an arm to her head slowly and winced when she touched the bump. Slowly she opened her eyes and looked up at Harris holding her. Groggy, she smiled a little and without saying a word, Harris gently put her feet down so she could stand, though he continued to hold her by the waist until she was steady.

"How do you feel?" I asked her, turning my attention back to the darkness ahead of us.

"Like I was run over by a freight train," she replied. It took her a moment to get her balance and soon she seemed to have her bearings about her. I smiled her direction but didn't take my eyes off our approach.

The lift was close to our level when out of the corner of my eye I noticed those same blue glowing eyes like beacons in the night. The creature was a ways off, but there was no telling how long it would be until it found us standing there.

"Over there!" I hissed through clenched teeth.

"Cogspit!" Harris spat and then looked up at the dial above the doorway to the elevator that showed the lift was still 20 floors above. "I don't think we're going to make it."

Eva squinted into the darkness and then wobbled on her feet slightly, having to grab my chair to steady herself. I reached up a hand to help her and looked to Harris for an idea of what to do.

"Let's hole up somewhere nearby and then make a mad break for it when the lift comes," he said.

"Alright, where to? I'll follow you and make sure Eva makes it."

Harris pointed to a small alley between two buildings a few doors down and without hesitation, he dashed over and shuffled out of sight. I pushed Eva ahead of me and she worked to make it over there. Once she was out of sight, I rolled my chair toward the opening. As I pushed, I heard a loud whoosh. Just before I rounded the corner, a massive black sinewed hand grabbed the back of my chair and spun me around. In front of me was a hulking creature from the things of nightmares. It's what I imagined a demon looks like, if it was a massive, ten-foot tall beast with arms and legs made of nothing but muscle, cloaked in black. Batlike wings spread several feet to either side of its barreled torso and a palpable darkness coiled around it like a mist. The face was vaguely human, but mostly Freddy Krueger-ish (yes, that's a word now. I panicked and that's what came to mind first). Where eyes should have been, there were simply two glowing blue orbs that appeared like fire and conveyed no emotion.

My heart probably stopped for a few seconds. Thankfully, I had enough presence of mind to yell "RUN!" but as I drew in a breath to scream, the beast reached out and put a grotesque large hand over my mouth to silence me. My eyes grew wide as I felt the leathery fingers wrap around the side and back of my head and pressed to stop my scream. I tried pulling backward, away from the Voidkin but with a hand grappling my head, there was nowhere for me to go.

A second Voidkin landed next to me and my heart, which was already trying to burst from my chest, kicked into overdrive and I started feeling lightheaded. The dark mist between the two monsters was thick and moist and I felt my skin prickle with every passing moment. Time seemed to slow and all of a sudden, all I could hear was my heartbeat pounding in my ears.

The monsters grabbed my arms and took to flight. It was not a smooth ride, either. They weren't flying in sync and it seemed like they had different ideas about where to take me, presumably to enjoy me for a mid-evening snack. I pulled against them, trying to break free but it was no use. They had me firm in their grasp and nothing was going to stop them from tearing me limb from limb. A few moments later, the Voidkin had flown me up several stories to a landing outside a building next to the elevator we had been waiting for earlier. I could see the elevator descending placidly without a care in the world down to where we had called it while the Voidkin dropped me on the landing and stood over me with a menacing scowl. Then again, truth be told, everything they did was menacing. A dull pain pulsed through my body as my back and arm seemed rather unhappy with being violently removed from the wheelchair, then dropped to the ground. What is it with me and falling painfully to the earth?

From the darkness between the Voidkin, a smaller figure stepped forward. A man who looked to be no more than 30 stood before me, a wistful grin on his face, his arms loosely crossed. He was exceedingly pale to the point of near translucent skin, so much so that even in the darkness I could see how pale he was, though that didn't belay how handsome he was. He wore a tight, jet black coat which fastened on his left flank by a few large silver buttons and had a small sturdy collar. The coat fanned out at the bottom and disappeared in the dark mist around him. Sharp features and short cropped hair whisked to the side made him seem commanding yet approachable. That is, until you glance at his piercing *red* eyes. The whites nearly blended in with his pale skin and bled into an altogether sinister red iris with black pupils. I gulped hard and determined that I was living out one of my own personal ideas of what hell would be like.

After a beat, the man pointed a slender finger at me and leaned in close to my face. His lips parted slightly and a cool, baritone honeyed voice said, "Finnegan Benjamin Riley, how nice to *finally* meet you."

Cogspit.

CHAPTER FOURTEEN

The chilling, macabre man in front of me with his hulking friends were giving my blood pressure a run for its money. My heart sank and I was pretty sure the soup from earlier was about to make its way back up. It probably would have, save for the massive black hand wrapped three quarters of the way around my face and covering my mouth.

The pale man continued, one eyebrow arched. "Oh yes, Finn, I know you. I know you, your family and your entire life. I know how you got here and I know *why* you're here." His red eyes flashed as he spoke, punctuating each of his remarks. His voice was unnervingly smooth but had a malevolent twist to it. He, too, had an accent, but this one was more South African than English proper.

"Now, I bet you have a load of questions and I'm sure we can get to those in time." He licked his lips like he was tasting more than the air around us. As his tongue passed over the skin, it momentarily looked rotten and decayed before resuming its pale features. "Before we get to that, though, I need to know where the shard is."

He rested a hand on the Voidkin's arm and it immediately released its grip on my mouth. He held a finger up on his other hand toward me and raised both eyebrows with a gesture of 'don't you dare scream or you'll regret it.' Yes, I definitely *wanted* to scream, but at this point my heart was beating so fast and my mouth was so completely dry that I wasn't sure I could make any sound, let alone a scream.

"Come now, Finnegan, I haven't got much time," he said, wiggling his finger impatiently.

I tried to speak but nothing came out. As a matter of fact, everything got so quiet I couldn't even hear my heartbeat anymore. I think I was getting tunnel vision or something because I couldn't hear or move or anything and the edges of my sight were getting blurry. Everything seemed to slow down too.

The pale man slowly turned his head and looked off to his right. In an instant, his expression shifted from impatient indifference to a twisted sneer and suddenly he vanished in a cloud of black mist. A moment later, the Voidkin whose arm had been wrapped around my head pitched forward, its face twisted in pain. The other Voidkin snarled and turned to its right and lunged behind the first Voidkin, arms outstretched. Behind them at the elevator stood Eva and Harris and with them, Giles and a few other people I didn't recognize. Giles held something resembling a long whip with barbs all along it and was in the process of reeling it back towards him from having lashed the Voidkin. Oh, and did I mention the whip was crackling with blue green *lightning*. Yeah.

Next to him, a shorter, rotund woman stood, feet spread and holding a gun. Well, no, I guess maybe not. I only got a quick look, but it looked more like the *exoskeleton* of a gun, if that were a thing. It didn't look completely whole, as the barrel was exposed to the air with a hole in the middle of it and the mechanisms were all outside the casing. She pulled the trigger once and a pellet of blue light cracked through the darkness and caught the other Voidkin between the eyes and its head snapped backward. It crumpled to the ground and a moment later, dissolved into dark mist.

Giles reared back once more and cast the whip out again. This time, the leather caught the creature along the leg and wrapped around it several times. A flash of light rippled through the weapon. The Voidkin's body tensed for a moment and something resembling steam rose off its flesh before it, too, turned to mist.

Clearing his throat, Giles recoiled the whip in one fluid motion and called out in his gruff voice, "Get in the lift, everyone. Now!"

Without missing a beat, Harris stepped back inside the elevator and pulled Eva along inside as well. The woman, with the two other younger men behind her, turned and walked a few paces to stand on alert in the carriage as well. Giles dashed over to me with surprising agility for a man his age and threw one arm under my good arm and heaved me to my feet.

"Lad, you're going to have to do some of the lifting this time," he said through clenched teeth, nearly dragging me toward the elevator shaft, my feet stumbling. With one arm under me and his whip still in his right hand, Giles heaved me into the elevator into the waiting arms of Harris and Eva. Immediately, he closed the gate and mashed the button for the top floor, level 82. He closed his eyes and placed a hand against the panel and small blue sparks rippled out from his fingers. At once, the elevator took to new speeds. The lift carriage looked like a well maintained elevator from the early to mid 1900s, with a metal frame and glass windows looking out on the city. The sides of the elevator car were a wrought metal with beautiful depictions of people and sunlight and a large wall with an intricate design on it. All told, it had a similar feel to the supply freighter from before.

I held on to Harris and Eva tightly, partly because I was terrified out of my mind from the Voidkin and that freaky pale guy, partly because I was startled by whatever the heck I'd just seen Giles and that other lady do, partly because we were about to be a living demonstration of the Tower of Terror ride in this elevator, and partly because I couldn't really stand or walk on my own.

No one spoke during the ride. The two young men and the woman with the gun stood looking intently out the glass panel, presumably to see through the darkness for anything that might come back for round two. They appeared to be trained military or somesuch. Or maybe not. I have no clue. Eva and Harris held me up and did their best to stay out of the way of her dad. Giles kept his eyes shut the entire trip and focused on whatever he was doing to the elevator to make it go so fast.

Altogether, the entire ride was probably 30 seconds? Maybe faster. I don't know or want to think much more about it. I'm pretty much over the whole "being thrown from something moving at obnoxious speeds to my impending doom" part of life. I didn't want it to be a part of life to begin with.

The lift slowed and came to a stop and Giles threw open the door with a slam. The others all filed out and headed down the hallway to several enormous metal doors which open slightly, let them in and then shut abruptly. Eva and Harris helped me out of the elevator and plopped me on a chair just outside the lift doors. Giles walked a few brisk steps down the hallway and then turned on his heel to face us.

"Father, we - " Eva began, but was interrupted by Giles throwing up a hand in a frustrated silencing gesture.

"Save it, Eva. Of all the foolish, bullheaded, idiotic ideas you've had, this one tops the list," he grumbled angrily. "You all could've been *killed* out there! When we spoke, I told you that under *no circumstances* were you to leave the Barrow. And you certainly weren't to come here." He stood there, one hand up and gesturing wildly as he spoke, the other firmly planted on his hip. "Kal would've looked after you lot while we got this under control. I can't believe he let you go. I'm going to have a word with him next time - "

This time it was Eva's turn to interrupt.

"Kal's gone dad. Everyone..." she paused, her voice catching in her throat. "We were going to stay, really. But as we waited, one of the Voidkin managed to get into the Network and find us down there. The people seeking shelter in the Barrow were killed and Kal bought us the time we needed to get out on the supply freighter. He saved us, dad."

Giles' expression changed at once and he swallowed hard.

Eva continued, "We had no choice. As soon as we got in the freighter, the Voidkin chased after us and even managed to get at us a few times." She turned slightly to show her still immensely swollen bump on her head.

"By the Ember, child!" Giles replied, his

gruff tone softening. He shifted over to her and investigated the swelling more carefully. "We need to get that swelling down quickly! Get down the hall to Cecilia and have her take care of you."

He hugged her tightly and then without a word ushered her down the hall. He then turned and looked at Harris.

"Mr. Archer, you've done so much for us already but would you be willing to escort Eva to Dr. Kilpatrick's?" Giles asked, eyes pleading with the young man.

Harris nodded and moved to catch up with Eva, sliding his arm through hers to help stabilize her as she walked.

Finally,Giles then turned and looked at me, squinting and tilting his head slightly.

"And you, young man. You're doubly lucky to be alive. I can see that the bandages I gave you are gone and you're wearing a tablecloth now. You're lucky the stitches didn't rip out or the Augs didn't just simply paralyze you the moment you left your bed." His tone was softer than it had been when we first got off the elevator but he still seemed frustrated.

I faked a smile and replied, "Well, it was either leave my bed or be eaten alive by a terrifying nightmare creature straight out of a Stephen King novel." I replied. Giles' frown deepened and I couldn't tell if he didn't like my joke, or just didn't get it.

"In any case," he continued, "hang tight and I'll have one of my assistants come and take care of you shortly. You seem well enough that I don't have to worry about you passing out on me again. I need to get back into the Council meeting or we may never be rid of those things, otherwise I'd take care of you myself." Giles motioned to the guards near the large doors the others had gone through and it clicked open.

"By the way," he continued as he turned to head through the door, "when this is all over, you and I are going to need to have a talk." That heavy tone returned to his voice once again.

"I think you're right," I shot back, a bit of an edge creeping into my voice. He waved a hand above his head in a "yeah, you bet" gesture and proceeded through the large metal doors that shut behind him.

I melted into the chair and let the silence and stillness center me. I took several deep breaths and worked to bring my heart rate back to normal. Left by myself and seemingly safe for the time being, it gave me a chance to take in my surroundings. Since the darkness had settled in, this was one of the only rooms in which the lights worked, aside from the Barrow earlier. The hallway I sat in was fairly mundane. There were polished marble floors with a carpeted floor runner heading from one end where the elevator was all the way down the hallway to the massive doors that Giles had left through. Just before those doors, however, was a hallway branching off to the right which I couldn't see down at this time.

There were a few side tables lining the corridor and a number of old ornate Victorian era portraits hanging on the walls, bordered by beautifully crafted golden frames. Most were of a member of the Council and had a small plaque beneath with the name of the person depicted. Ultimately, they were all too far away for me to read the inscriptions and there was no way I was getting up from this chair.

A few other paintings hung in the hallway as well, closer to where I sat. Across the hall from me, one picture in particular caught my eye. It was a scene of what appeared to be a volcano and a huge wall, similar to the relief in the elevator. This picture, though, had a bright light on the volcano and a terrifying dark face off in the distance, nearly the size of the mountain itself. The plaque beneath stated "The Culling."

On the wall just above me and to my right was a detailed schematic. In the top right corner, the words "The Territories of the United People of the Emberwall." The depiction had the look of a blueprint, though it was colored and incredibly detailed. A compass rose was etched in the bottom right hand corner indicating "north." To the east, there seemed to be a sharp and clearly defined line that cut diagonally across the schematic from the top to the bottom. None of the territories passed this line and the words scrawled in calligraphy along the line simply stated Emberwall. At the northern edge, topography detailed that the Obsidian Mountain Range began. The schematic cut off just past the start of the mountain on the northern side. Along the west and southern edge, it looked like someone had drawn large tendrils licking out from the edge of the city schematics with the word "Embervein" on each.

The rest of the blueprint detailed twelve Wards, which I guess are like districts, each with a separate name and color pattern. On the bottom of the depiction appeared a brief description:

"It is hereby declared that the territories of the people of Emberwall be evenly and equally distributed by square-foot to the parties aforementioned. Territory constituents may use their allotment in the fashion their peoples deem most appropriate and will in no way encroach on the neighboring territories. Each territory will select one citizen to be the representative for their Ward to convene the Proterezar, the governance of the Twelve territories of the United People of Emberwall. Selection of each delegate, heretoforth "Ekorius" will be determined by the individual Wards and will not be infringed upon by the Proterezar itself. Together, the city of Emberwall stands united. Together, the darkness shall not prevail. May the Arcmagus guide us."

"Well, at least that explains what this Council is," I mused out loud to myself. Having taken a moment to compose myself, I mulled over the events of the day in an attempt to make some sense of what was going on. Chief complaint I needed answered was who the blazes that creepy guy was and how did he know who I was? And what are the Voidkin? They're certainly not human and I've never seen anything like it except in horror movies. It took everything in me to not retch just thinking about them. I don't even know where to begin with Harris and Giles shooting sparks from their hands and electricity crackling through whips and guns.

We're definitely not in Kansas anymore, Toto.

All the questions without answers were starting to give me a headache, so instead I closed my eyes and focused on breathing, ignoring the pain dully washing over my whole body.

CHAPTER FIFTEEN

I felt a gentle tap on my shoulder. I opened my eyes and saw a young lady in a teal blue dress and a white cap standing next to me with a wheelchair, similar to the one from earlier.

"We're ready to take you now, Mr. Finn," she said softly, smiling down at me, her voice light and airy.

"Oh okay," I replied in a whisper. I don't know why I felt like I needed to whisper. Maybe because there was no one around and it seemed like such a serious place.

"My name is Katherine and I'll be caring for you today. I know you are probably in a lot of pain based on what Dr. Fleming told me, so just take it easy and we'll have you taken care of in no time, alright?" She had a charming cheerfulness in her voice which no doubt came from years of practice, putting patients at ease as they're about to undergo intense and painful surgery.

With her help, I was easily able to shuffle into the wheelchair. She pushed me down the long corridor and I got a better look at the portraits of the Council members. We continued towards the massive doors of the Council chamber and then took the right hand turn down the hallway Eva and Harris had gone down before. We passed by several rooms which looked to be conference rooms or sitting areas. The chairs and tables and all of the decorations had an antique look about them. The Council must have really liked the industrial chic decor choices. Everywhere we went, the furniture had metal wrought through it, interlaced with dark wood which, all together, made for a rather beautiful scene. We passed several rooms with closed doors until we reached a small room where the door was propped open. An examination table sat ready for use in the center of the room, and looked similar to the room where Giles worked on me several days ago. There was an odd combination of mechanical tools and medical instruments lining the walls and tables. It didn't look so much like a doctor's office as it did a sterile machine shop.

Nurse Katherine wheeled me over to the table and helped me onto my stomach to lie on the table and gently peeled back my robe. She worked quietly and methodically, trying to make sure I was comfortable and seemed to be succeeding. She gently slipped a pair of medical shears under the makeshift bandage Harris had thrown together at the Barrow and deftly sliced through the material. I felt the cool edge of the metal blade against my skin and it sent a pleasant shiver down my back. She set down the shears and then set about pulling individual strips of the bandage off until my back was exposed. The nurse turned and set down the wad of bandages and then turned back to examine my wounds. Just then, she let out a small gasp and brought a hand to her mouth.

"What is it?" I asked, concernedly.

Her voice became detached and calm in that way medical professionals tend to, but I swear I heard it quiver slightly. "Dr. Flemming mentioned that you would have... extensive restructuring damage and that we would probably need to repair most of your spine, torso and arms at this point."

"Yeah, so what's the damage? Am I going to

be on bed rest for the next sixty years of my life?" I asked, sarcastically, trying to make light of the fact that the nurse just freaking *gasped* after looking at me.

"Uhhh, I need to check something," she said, and hurried out of the room.

"Nurse?" I called out. "Hey! Wait! What's going on?"

Well this is fun. I love when people look at me and then run away in terror. Definitely a *confidence booster*. I'm feeling REALLY good right now about my prospects in the future.

Thankfully, a few moments later the nurse returned, Harris and Giles with her. Giles looked frustrated, probably from being pulled from the Council chamber *yet again* because of me. The three of them came to my side and looked at my back.

"By the Ember!" Giles muttered.

"I didn't really understand what you had instructed doctor, except for the patterning that is..." Katherine trailed off and didn't really seem to know what else to say.

"Harris, you bandaged him up earlier this evening, right?" Giles asked, turning to the young man.

"Mmhmm," he replied, nodding his head

and not offering up much more by way of response. His eyes were wide, though, and it was clear something was off.

"Would someone please tell me what is going on?!" I demanded.

Giles took a deep breath. "Lad. You remember how long I worked on you and what I did to put you back together, yes?"

I nodded fervently and beckoned for him to continue. I just wanted him to get to the point.

"Well, that kind of damage needs months to heal and years to rehabilitate, if it's ever going to heal at all."

"Yeah, I remember you telling me that and then being confronted with the fact that my life as I knew it was pretty much over. And then I was attacked by some spawn of Satan. So I kinda came to terms with my physical predicament when I was face to face with death incarnate!" I said, dripping with sarcasm as best as I possibly could.

"Just give it to me straight, doc," I said, shifting my tone to a more serious bent.

Giles walked over to one of the side tables and grabbed several objects from a drawer. He came back to where I was and handed me a mirror. He held another one up pointed down at my back.

"Take a look, lad."

I held up the mirror in such a way that I could see the one in his hand and in turn, my own back.

Now it was my turn to gasp. I could *feel* the pain and the stitches pulling on my skin. I saw the bruising earlier in the Barrow, wrapping around my side and arm. What I saw in the mirror, though, was nothing but smooth unblemished skin, save for a faint pink scar that wrapped from my shoulder down to the middle of my back like forks of lightning. I followed the scar with my eyes and it wrapped around my shoulder and then twisted down my arm to my forearm, ending in a small triangle at the base of my wrist.

Up to now, I had been afraid to turn or move much, except when it had been absolutely necessary for fear of pulling out the stitches. Seeing me now, I decided to chance it. I twisted and propped myself up on my "good" arm. A small, dull ache pulsed through my body, but nothing like that crippling waves of sharp pain I'd experienced earlier. I couldn't hide my astonishment and by the looks on their faces, neither could they.

"*What happened to me?*" I asked, the sarcasm gone, replaced with confusion.

"I think we need to have that conversation *now*, lad," Giles replied, his face a mask of emotion.

I nodded and forced myself to sit all the way up. It hurt, but it felt more like I had gone through a really intense workout and my muscles were sore. Occasional jabs of pain shot through my side and my back, but it was still significantly better than it had been even just an hour earlier. I reached over and grabbed the robe from the side table and slipped it on while we spoke.

"Katherine, please give us a few minutes," Giles asked the nurse, putting a hand on her arm.

She nodded once, still not taking her eyes off of me. She lingered a moment longer and then headed for the door.

"Oh, and Katherine?" Giles offered.

She turned to look as her hand reached the doorknob.

"Please don't mention this to anyone, my dear. It would be premature to share without knowing more of the story," Giles said gently with a slight smile.

"Of course, sir. I cannot break the confidentiality of my patient, sir," she replied, almost robotically and then exited quickly.

"Well, then," Giles said as he turned back to

me. Harris stepped next to the both of us, still seemingly glazed from the whole situation.

"We'd best get to talking, lad."

CHAPTER SIXTEEN

Giles pulled up a stool alongside the examination table and Harris leaned against the counter across from me. They were both quiet. I spoke first.

"So, as much as I want and, frankly, *need* answers for all of this, let's start with the scary demon things. These Voidkin, has anything like this happened ever?"

"Not in any recent memory," Giles replied, stretching his neck and rubbing it with one hand.

"Why now? Have you guys been able to figure out what is causing the darkness or why the Voidkin showed up now?"

"The Proterezar is still in discussion on the matter, but as far as anyone knows, the only way the Void would be able to overtake our city like this is if someone brought it about…" His voice trailed off momentarily and he seemed distant. He shook his head, apparently clearing his thoughts and then proceeded.

"The Void isn't able to go anywhere the Ember is. The city rests on a humongous Embervein which flows from the Wall. An event happened generations ago which pushed back the Void to where it could not overtake the Ember. We don't have time for a history lesson, but basically at the time, the Void threatened to take over the entire world and the last bastion of hope was the Emberwall and the small city that rested at the foot of the wall. From that point forward, the Void could not go anywhere near the Emberveins and we've been safe ever since."

He folded his arms across his chest and leaned on the stool, contemplatively. Harris' smooth voice chimed in, "So then, how did it get here now?"

"Someone had to have brought it here. They would have to usher it over the Ember by some means we aren't quite sure of. It isn't entirely clear how one would go about doing that if it were even possible," Giles ruminated to himself.

"But that would be really difficult, I assume?" I asked.

"Incredibly. But in theory, if someone had enough control of Lusynos, that would possibly be enough to summon the Void. The real question is *why*."

"Well, who do you know that might have enough power to do that?" Harris asked.

"A few of the members of the Council, possibly. A few in the aristocracy may also be able but only if they worked together and I don't know why any of them would want to bring the Void here to terrorize the world. There's nothing to be gained from that."

"Okay, okay, hang on," I interjected. "What is this Lusynos you're talking about?"

Giles turned to face me and glowered. "Gah, I keep forgetting that you don't know anything."

Well that's kind of rude. But then again, I *don't* know anything, so I suppose he's right. I kept my mouth shut and tried not to look offended while Giles continued.

He grabbed the whip attached to his hip and unfurled it. "There are two overarching powers in our world. Lusynos and Adrinyn. The former is a lot less common and generally unwelcome in our society. Lusynos is an innate power to control the world around you through means of matter manipulation and displays of power. It usually requires some kind of focus, like a ring or a wand or an amulet to channel. In general, people don't like Lusynos for the very reason that it is able to tap into some unseen power and perform feats of incredible strength.

"With that kind of power, there is no way to keep tabs on what someone might do with it and so anyone displaying any kind of prowess with Lusynos from a young age is registered and is not allowed to practice the art, except under strict supervision. Society as a whole is incredibly skeptical of the use of Lusynos and so most people who display any kind of aptitude for it don't train in it anyway because they don't want to be an outcast.

"The second kind of power in our world is Adrinyn. It's similar to Lusynos, but much more restrictive. If you've noticed, our world is heavily reliant on machinery. Transportation, buildings, workforce, everything in some way or shape is influenced by machinery. Adrinyn gives the user the ability to augment machinery beyond what we might be able to accomplish with only tools. It is

how we built Emberwall into such a prominent
city. It's how I was able to make the lift up here
travel at such high speed."

Harris chimed in, "And how I was able to
manipulate our freighter to go so fast."

Giles gave him an approving look. "So you
see, lad, we can use the manipulation of
electromagnetic fields and mechanical parts to go
beyond average uses. Anyone using Adrinyn
though, can't simply snap it into being out of thin
air. All users have some kind of augmentation to
their body which aides them in channeling
Adrinyn. These are called Augs and you," as he
pointed a finger at me, "are riddled with them
now."

I looked at my hand and arm, surprised.
Giles continued.

"The mechanical pieces I worked into your
system to keep you alive a few weeks back were all
a variant of my own design on the standard
augmentation biomes. Most people wielding
Adrinyn simply have something they clip on or
wear to help them channel." He motioned to Harris
and Harris pulled up his left pant leg and to reveal
an ornate metal brace around his calf. A mixture of
cogs and sprockets linked together to form a cast

around much of his lower leg. He then pulled up the sleeve on his right arm and a similar device covered his forearm, almost to his wrist.

Giles continued, "These are fairly standard augs, though many people have variations on the theme. You'll often see someone with an arm or a leg aug working in industry, because it helps them channel Adrinyn through those extremities to give them a boost. Consequently, Harris can channel through his hands and his legs to help him while he is working in the shop with the other boys. He also uses it when he helps me in the operation theater." Harris readjusted his clothing and settled back against the counter again.

"My job is to help reconstruct patients who have been injured and lost the use of something skeletal in nature. I create augs for them and then surgically implant them to replicate the lost limb or body part and to function like normal. It's a form of biomedical augmentation and has become fairly commonplace here in Emberwall over the last generation or so. Most of these are not designed to allow the patient to wield Adrinyn, but simply to reconstruct from injuries. I have a few of these myself which I modified to open channels for me to use Adrinyn. The ones I worked into you were standard augs which don't enable channeling and were simply reconstructive implants to help you function like normal."

At this, he flicked his whip out and it unfurled across the floor gently. It was a long piece of leather, interlaced with malleable metal which swirled across the leather in a beautiful design, The whip itself was rather stunning as a piece of art. A moment later, Giles hand flashed blue and that same blue-green flash of electricity crackled down the whip along the curls of metal.

"And while it isn't often necessary, Adrinyn can come in handy for militaristic uses as well." The whip teemed with sparks of electricity until Giles motioned with his hand and the crackling stopped.

"Whoa. Okay, that was awesome," I replied, staring openly at the whip.

"One of the defining characteristics of the Council members is their ability with either Adrinyn or Lusynos. We are all fairly powerful users and are chosen to help guide the direction of the city because of our unique ability to control these elements," Giles continued, recoiling his whip and clipping it back to his belt.

"Most of us simply go on with our daily

lives and have normal jobs and function as regular members of society. But every so often we gather together in moments of crisis or when there is a semi-annual council meeting to help make sure the citizens of Emberwall are protected and they're growing in a healthy direction as a society. Most Wards have their own small governmental groups and all of us are on those councils as well."

"So, then in this circumstance, who might be most equipped to summon the Void like this?" I asked.

"We haven't been able to come to a conclusion. We were just discussing that when Lydia and I came down to help you. So that brings me to my questions for *you* Finn," Giles said, leaning forward on his stool and staring directly at me.

"You fell into our lives shortly before this chaos, a secret we've kept close to the chest. And while I don't believe you're the cause, it is suspicious that you have come at such a time. That said, lad, you've also had the misfortune of being chased by Voidkin throughout the evening. From talking with Harris a little while ago, it seems to me that they could have killed you several times. Instead, they waited until you were alone, then swooped in and seized you. Instead of killing you, they made off with you. Now, tales I've heard about the Voidkin are usually about death and destruction, not retrieve and capture," Giles said as he moved closer to me, lowering his voice and staring intently.

"My job right now is to make sure that the city is safe. I'm not able to do that very well if I don't have all the information. So tell me, Finn, why didn't they kill you?" His expression was stern and cold and his demeanor had shifted to stone. His bright blue eyes seemed darker and his entire posture seemed like a brooding storm about to break.

I tried to look calm, but truthfully, I was sweating and racking my brain for answers. Heat rose in my face.

"I don't know," I replied, quietly. I felt like a little kid again, getting in trouble with dad and being scrutinized for something I didn't do. "When those things grabbed me and flew me up to that landing, a creepy guy appeared and asked me something about a shard. He knew who I was, called me out by name and he claimed to know why I was here," I offered.

Giles took in a long breath and mulled it

over for a solid minute.

"That's troubling," Giles finally said as his forehead furrowed. "I'm not sure who he was, but we're aware of creatures of the Void that are more apt and dangerous than the Voidkin, though no one has ever come in contact with them. We've only had sparse interactions with the Voidkin to begin with and never something this openly confrontational. Any expeditions we've ever sent outside the Embervein have been unsuccessful."

"Well, I wish I had more to offer, but I don't. I'm more in the dark about all of this than you seem to be," I mused.

I shifted uncomfortably on the examination table and looked around the room. Strange contraptions lined the walls and tables. Tools and medical instruments intermixed and glinted in the sterile light of the room. I sighed and looked to Harris and Giles who both seemed deep in thought.

"So what do we do now?" I asked, trying to shift the focus from me to something else. Their explanation helped me understand a little bit better what was going on, but I didn't know why or how I had become a part of it.

"I'm not sure. The Council is going to need

more information if we are going to combat this threat. There isn't anything we can do against the Void without knowing what brought them here in the first place."

Harris chimed in, "What would that take?"

"It's more a matter of narrowing down who might have been able to summon the Void and then seeking them out, ruling them out one by one. We have some teams out now who were tasked with finding a few people but none of them have returned yet. Communications are down or at least severely limited, save for direct lines that are hardwired into the mainframe, so it is taking longer than we had hoped."

Silence filled the room. Harris looked lost in thought and Giles's furrowed expression left little room for discussion. I didn't really know how to engage, so I steered toward a different question.

"How about my injuries. Is there some explanation that might lead to why or how I recovered so quickly?"

Giles shook his head. "In all my years working to rebuild broken bodies, I've never seen anything like this. You were recovering adequately back at my house. In the last two weeks, I'd say your body was healing only slightly faster than normal. I checked up on your progress two or three days ago.." he said, trailing off as he thought about it.

Harris interjected. "And you were bruised and scabbed at the Barrow. Your stitches were pretty bloody and that was only a few hours ago. There weren't that many open wounds, though, considering how much blood you lost at the Fleming's when Eva and I found you."

"That kind of healing just shouldn't be possible!" Giles said, his gruff voice a mixture of confusion and excitement.

Just then, a young man with coiffed hair and a dark military style jacket like the ones I saw earlier poked his head around the corner and cleared his throat.

"Dr. Fleming, the Council is requesting your presence immediately."

"Very well, Simon. Thank you," Giles nodded to the young man who immediately excused himself. Giles slapped his hands against his knees in a gesture of resolution.

"Well, I guess the rest will have to wait, gentlemen. Finn, when this is all over, we'll run some tests and see if we can't figure out what's going on with your body. As it stands, I would take it as a blessing from the Ember and carry on. It seems like it's going to be a very long evening." Giles offered, pushing himself up with his hands and moving to the doorway. He paused for a moment and then turned back to face us.

"Actually, would you be interested in joining? You lads are the only successful group to get here from beyond this Ward and you might know more than you think. I can't guarantee the Council will need you, but at this point it wouldn't hurt to have another few sets of ears. We've been at this a while and not much closer to having a solution."

Harris and I looked at each other, shrugged and got up to join him. I gingerly hopped off the examination table and moved to the wheelchair. As I walked, though, the pain was even less than before and I felt more confident about my body. I sidestepped the chair and decided to muscle my way down the hallway. Both other men in gave a nod of approval and we headed out.

CHAPTER SEVENTEEN

It was a long, difficult walk back down the hallway. My muscles were definitely atrophied but I wasn't about to take any moment of movement for granted. My legs gave out from under me a few times and Harris had to catch me to make sure I didn't split my head open on the wall or floor. It was slow going, but we finally made it back down the hall toward the ornate doorway leading into the Council chamber.

As we walked, Eva emerged from a room on our left with a small bandage wrapped around her head and a cold pack she held against her injury. We looked at each other in astonishment. Her mouth hung open for a moment, looking me up and down and then she fumbled for some words.

"You're walking!" She exclaimed. "How -"

"Not sure, but no time right now to figure it out," I replied, holding tightly onto Harris' arm and shuffling my way down the hall.

"I didn't realize how tall you were," she mused, her accent rounding out the words with a sense of genuine curiosity.

"Well, it makes fitting into small spaces a pain, but I've come to terms with it," I rattled off, focused on the task of making it from point A to point B.

The four of us made it down the hallway and finally reached the large doors to the Council chamber. The door clicked open at a wave of Giles' hand and the guards standing to either side pulled open the massive metal door.

Giles strode into the room and Harris helped me through the doorway while Eva came in last and the door shut behind us.

As we entered, I tried to take in all the sights without looking too much like a tourist on his first trip to Disneyland. The chamber was a large hollow room stretching roughly sixty feet upward, give or take. The space was mostly dominated by large windows which were built on an angle leading inward to a point. The center of the roof was a glass belfry with a large mission bell hanging proudly above the city. The walls beneath the windows were tall and were interlaced with mechanical gears throughout. The entire room reminded me of what I imagine the inside of Big Ben is like in London, if the gears were on the walls. Any wall space which wasn't occupied by mechanics was layered with beautiful burnished bronze which glistened with the light from the room. Along the walls were sconces in a similar industrial fashion which housed open-air Edison bulbs every two feet or so which lit up the room nicely. There were stadium seats lining the outside of the hall which worked downward to a center stage-like area with an oblong boardroom table littered with papers and small objects. Looming just beyond the stage in the center of the room was a platform. A second long table of ornate dark wood held thirteen intricate chairs which faced the stage, giving the feeling of a large, intense courtroom scene. The upper platform was empty, however, and everyone in the room was focused around the boardroom table, all embroiled in the work of trying to solve the crisis at hand.

With the sound of the door closing, a few of the Council members looked up. I recognized a few from their portraits on the wall, but couldn't remember any names from their plaques.

"Giles, thank goodness. We think we've made a breakthrough," a heavier set woman said as she looked up from her work. I recognized her as the woman who helped Giles take out the Voidkin earlier. The gun was still clipped to her belt in a strange holster and her curly brown hair was tousled haphazardly.

"What've you got, Lydia?" he asked, striding quickly across the room from the entry to the table, glancing at the papers scattered about.

An older gentleman, probably in his early sixties looked up from a document he was reading and glanced over his spectacles at Giles. He was wearing high waisted dark grey pants tucked into his large boots with the flaps turned down and a black double-breasted jacket which opened in the front but flowed in tails long in the back. His face was slim and gaunt and wrinkles touched his eyes and cheeks. The glasses resting on his nose pinched the brow of his nose instead of wrapping around his ears. All told, he gave me the impression of an undertaker or an Ichabod Crane impersonator.

The gentleman cleared his throat and engaged Giles, his voice high pitched and shrill. "It appears that there has been a bit of an error in our original theory. We missed a key detail." His voice had a clipped old-world English accent and it just somehow fit his entire persona. He extended a thin, lanky arm toward Giles with the document he had been reading a moment earlier. The page looked as though it had been torn from a book, the edges jagged. Giles glanced down at the sheet as the man continued speaking.

"Yes, well, we knew that this sort of phenomenon was not within the boundaries of the natural order and would need someone wielding Lusynos with a substantial amount of power to push the Void beyond the Embervein." He paused a moment, allowing Giles to read over the page. Other members of the Council continued in silence as they scoured the pages on the table for more information.

Undertaker McScaryface continued, "Well, August managed to secure this information from one of the older editions of the Arcmanion -"

A much younger man, probably in his late twenties or early thirties looked up from his work and his face lit up. His blond hair draped in front of his face and with a motion, he brushed it aside and chimed in.

"And we hadn't thought about it until now!" He was excited and burst with energy. Like Eva and Harris, the young man had only a faint accent. His chipper persona, though, trumped any other trait I could describe. The guy was like a barely contained explosion of energy and personality. Next to him, the old man scowled for being interrupted but allowed the younger man to continue.

"It does take a user of considerable ability to complete a ritual this intensive, but there is absolutely no way he could do it alone." August said as he rushed to Giles' side and pointed at the sheet still in Giles' hand. Eva, Harris and I all moved closer behind Giles' shoulder to see what the fuss was about.

August continued, rocking back and forth on his feet, "That means that there would have to be *multiple* users, all continuously channeling Lusynos with the intent to open a way for the Void to breach the city. We still don't know who, but there is no doubt that it couldn't have been just one person!" His green eyes lit up with excitement, clearly excited at this find.

Over Giles' shoulder, I saw a diagram drawn on the page they had been passing around.

It depicted a group of hooded figures encircling a table with various items on it, like a lamp, a skull, a vial of something and a few other items. The text beneath the diagram was written in a script I couldn't understand, either because it was horrible handwriting or it was an entirely different language altogether. Giles nodded slightly to himself as he looked at the diagram and listened to August and the old man explain what they had found.

"Can we reverse it or stop it altogether?" Giles asked, a hand on his chin, stroking pensively at his beard.

"We're still narrowing that down, but there must be a way," August offered. "A ritual of this magnitude would need to be channeled for quite some time. The Arcmanion where I found the diagram was tattered and missing a generous amount of pages. We are hoping that another of the older manuscripts from the Athenaeum might have _"

Just then, another massive crash sounded off in the distance and the room began to shake. Everything not bolted down clattered. I nearly lost my balance and had to hold onto the table. The others grabbed onto whatever was nearest and waited for the shaking to stop. The sensation was a lot like what I felt at the house earlier but this time it was more focused and intense.

The Council members looked at each other and no one spoke. A few moments passed and the shaking subsided. Lydia pressed her hands to the table and breathed a sigh of relief. She straightened the sheets of parchment in front of her and then turned to August, Giles and the older man.

"We still don't know where Ekorius Thornsby is. No one has been able to reach him yet and I fear the worst with what's out there," Lydia said, a quiver in her voice as she spoke. She seemed rather sophisticated and her voice was slightly less bubbly than her appearance let on. There was a perpetual seriousness about her and she seemed to be occupied completely with the situation at hand. I imagine if I had met her in different circumstances, I might think otherwise.

Giles and the older man looked at each other. Something passed between them but I couldn't figure out if it was concern or something deeper.

"Elston, have we sent anyone to fetch Galen?" Giles asked the older man.

Of course his name was *Elston*. Only thing better would be Archibald or Thurston. It definitely fit his demeanor, that's for sure.

"Naturally," Elston replied, shrill and curt, his expression matching the reply.

"Well then, has there been any word from the team?" Giles shot back, exasperated.

"No. And I'm assuming there won't be," Elston droned. "None of the teams we have sent out have reported back and I'm working on the assumption that they've all perished or have been incapacitated at this time."

"Cogswallup!" Giles roared. "What kind of a leader are you? One of the Council is still out there and there hasn't been contact for several hours! Men and women you've sent out to do their jobs but haven't come back or checked in and you simply write them off as dead?"

He rubbed a hand across his face and slammed it down on the table. "And you expect that we're going to be able to somehow just magically stop the Void from overtaking our entire city until there's no one left except us by sitting here in this tower?"

Giles was seething, his eyes shooting daggers through Elston. The older man merely stared back with the same cool, puckered expression he'd been showing this entire time. I thought for a moment that a small smirk touched his lips, but he was so old and wrinkled that it was genuinely hard to tell.

Giles continued, his rage bubbling over, "You have a lot of nerve, Elston Blackwell. When this is all over -"

Lydia threw her hands up to either side and interrupted Giles mid-rant. "Gentlemen, please! The city is counting on us to solve this issue as quickly as possible or more people are going to die."

Giles took a deep breath and sat down on one of the short backed stools tucked under the table. "You're right, I'm sorry."

Elston merely continued to stare down Giles and after a moment, turned his attention back to the papers on the table in front of him.

I leaned over to Harris and whispered, "That guy seems like a walking skeleton with the personality to match."

A smile crept up Harris' mouth but he remained quiet and said nothing. He glanced over at me with a 'oh, totally,' look and then turned his attention back to Lydia who was readying for another attack.

"Now here's what we know," she started, a

southern American accent cresting her voice. "It has been 3 hours and forty two minutes since the darkness descended. The first quake was seven minutes after the darkness and the first known attack from the forces of the Void was an hour and twelve minutes after the darkness. It was not long before attacks were reported citywide from citizens who had a direct line to the mainframe. It seems likely that there were even more attacks than reported, since most people simply communicate by messorium. That said, we have a serious crisis on our hands.

"It stands to reason that whoever has invited the Void across our lands is still channeling the Lusynos necessary to accomplish such a feat, due to the diligent work of our dear young Ekorius Horus." August smiled and nodded once.

Lydia continued, "None of our search and rescue parties have come back from the Thornsby estate to retrieve Ekorius Thornsby, nor from the other Wards where we needed to ascertain the whereabouts of the most prominent Lusynos users. We cannot confirm nor deny at this point that these teams are safe or have met resistance from the Void forces. In addition, the only successful party to have made it any significant distance beyond their home is the young trio from Dr. Fleming's estate out in the Etherborough Ward. His estate rests on the far reaches of the outermost Embervein and we know for a fact that his residence has been cleared of all personnel and his daughter, as well as two young gentlemen are here to share what they know." She unfurled her arms and gestured to the three of us.

The Council members all looked up from their work and looked at us. A few of the council members seemed genuinely surprised at our presence. I don't think they had noticed that we came in with Giles and you could see the gears working in their heads to figure out why we had been invited in.

"Gentlemen, if you please. Dr. Fleming has indicated that there may be some important details that you have which could aid us in stopping this threat."

Harris coughed slightly and glanced over at me, eyebrows up and giving me a 'you go first,' look. I looked back, trying to give him a 'what?! No, I don't think so' look, but apparently that wasn't good enough because Giles grabbed me by the shoulder and started in for me.

"Finn here is a guest of mine..." he said,

pulling me closer to his side. I drew in a sharp breath as my body kicked into gear. I am definitely *not* all better yet. "...and he had a very strange experience just before getting here." He turned and looked at me, signaling me to start talking.

"Yeah, uhh, well..."I cleared my throat, it suddenly having become incredibly dry and began again. "So we were pursued by a Voidkin from Dr. Fleming's home all the way over here. We managed to secure transportation on a supply freighter and Harris here," I thumbed over towards him, "er, Mr. Archer, I mean, was able to get us to the station here pretty quickly. On the way, several more Voidkin attacked the freighter and we barely made it out alive. That said, just before we reached the elevator, er...lift... to come up here, two Voidkin swooped down and grabbed me and took me to a landing on a different level."

The Council members listened intently as I recounted the story. Many of them leaned forward, taking in every detail.

"They took me to an outcropping on a building and dropped me there and out of the darkness some creepy *really* pale guy dressed in all black appeared and talked with me. Before I could have much conversation with him, Dr. Fleming and this kind lady here stepped in and attacked the Voidkin to help me get away. After that, we zipped on up here and here we are."

There was a brief moment of silence as I finished and then Elston's shrill voice cut in. I almost winced as he spoke. "You mean to tell me that the Voidkin simply apprehended this young fellow and then a Felmaven just *talked* to him?" His voice was dripping with incredulity and disbelief.

"No, there is no way." Elston shook his head and crossed his arms. "I just simply don't believe it."

Lydia shot him a glance that could've killed a small animal. "Well *believe it*, Elston," She said as her southern accent punctuated every word, clearly irritated with the man.

"Giles and I both saw the Voidkin and something else between the two before we opened fire on them. We weren't about to let them devour this young man and so we didn't exactly stop to ask questions."

Ekorius Blackwell sat up straight and glared back, but said nothing in reply.

A tall, slender woman with long brown hair, in a golden dress with red shapes writhing throughout stood, raising a finger to politely interject.

"Ah, yes, Ekorius Percipity Emerson. The floor is yours." Lydia offered with a gesture toward the woman.

"If it truly was a Felmaven, we can no longer sit by studying our books. Quick action is necessary or the entire city is in immediate peril." Her voice was surprisingly deep and smooth, but still feminine.

"Percipity is right!" another Council member added. This man, a short, wiry fellow with an eccentric outfit of a bright rich blue from head to toe, stood out from the rest in his attire because his did not seem to reflect the same kind of style that everyone else did. I was sensing a Victorian theme among the fashion styles of the people of in this city, but this man was dressed entirely differently. He wore a more modern style of suit, but it was far too large for his frame. He couldn't have been more than 5'3" and weighed maybe a buck twenty five. He had to constantly push up the sleeves of the jacket for his hands to even stick out. The shirt he wore was the only matching attire to everyone else - white and billowy linen and puffing out of every hole or spot it possibly could. The shirt was held back by a vest of the same blue as the rest of his suit and it was in a word, awesome. His hair was going everywhere and reminded me of a young Albert Einstein, with dark brown hair and a carefree appearance.

At this declaration, the Council broke out into boisterous conversation about what to do and how to fix the problem. Everyone spoke over the top of one another and nothing was getting accomplished. Perhaps thirty seconds or so passed and Eva, Harris and I simply looked to one another and shrugged.

Finally, the tall woman from before slammed a fist down on the boardroom table and everyone abruptly stopped talking.

"We aren't getting anywhere and time is precious!" Her smooth voice streamed out like warm butter, but there was a firm edge to her tone.

"We need to find Galen and we need to find the perpetrators and stop this nonsense at once. Our most skilled teams have neglected to check in and for the time being we must assume the worst. We shall thank the Ember if, when this night is over, they return to us safely but for now we must continue as if they will not. I say we vacate the chambers except for a small band of us who will remain behind to monitor for any call-ins. The rest of the council should split up into teams and investigate the most important venues. As the Proterezar, it is our duty to exercise our talents to not only lead these people but to protect them. If our expert teams have been unsuccessful, we must assume the mantle ourselves," she continued.

"Very well then," Elston's stringy voice cut in. "I will stay here and monitor. Along with Kingsley and you, Percipity."

The strange little man in blue nodded and Percipity raised an assenting hand, palm up.

Giles chimed in next, "August, myself and Lydia will head for Thornsby. If he is injured, I'll be the most apt to help him." He got to his feet, adjusting his jacket.

"Ferris, Nan, Upton, Simone and Felicity, are you alright to set out to the last known locations of our 'most-wanted' list of Lusynos wielders?" Giles asked, turning to the other Council members standing by. "You're welcome to stick together or split up."

They nodded and immediately went about gathering their jackets and other belongings. They all seem loaded for bear, collecting up knives, swords, guns and a few other strange looking implements that didn't make sense to me. Frankly,

I was simply impressed with how quickly the team went from bickering and arguing to concluding a direction to go and simply picking up without hesitation. Perhaps there was something to be said for their leadership after all.

"Each team should check in as soon as they've made contact or reached their destination," Giles said, his eyes scanning the room as he prepared himself. "More communication is always better, and we're going into this without much information. Check in often and don't do anything that might get you killed. Try to stay off the trams and take surface streets as often as possible. Mass transport is not reliable and we know from the kid's trek here that the Voidkin are out and about near the Lightrail. Use the Network to get around if need be, it seems to be the safest."

I stood back and watched Giles giving instructions. He really knew how to command a room and it seemed he was actually in charge of the entire Council.

"Make sure you have each other's backs and, everyone..." he said, putting a firm hand out in front of him like a stop-sign. "...come back safe."

I looked around the room and everyone's eyes were on him, steeled and intense. The excitement in the air was palpable, but not without a hint of reservation. From the sound of it, this sort of expedition had never been necessary and this crew, while formidable from the looks of things, didn't seem like they'd done much by way of battling nightmarish flying creatures from the Void.

A moment passed and Giles' words hung in the air. Then, as if on cue, everyone grabbed the remainder of their belongings and headed out the large metal doors.

Giles turned to go first, strapping on a dark vest and shrugged into a thick leather duster. His whip was easily accessible through the front of the duster and he also had a small gun at his hip. He slung an army-green pack over his head and across his shoulders. On the front flap, a dark green cross was embroidered on the pack, and I assumed it was his medical supplies.

As he marched toward the doorway, he passed the three of us, standing to the side, allowing the Council members to exit the building.

Eva turned to her dad, bouncing a little on the balls of her feet.

"What about us dad?" She asked, rocking back and forth on her toes in excitement.

"You lot are going to stay here where it's

safe," Giles said, a hand outstretched toward us as he spoke.

"I'm not about to put you into any more danger and this is going to be a very dangerous job. You've already been hurt once today and your mother would never forgive me if I allowed you to get harmed on some foolhardy errand you're not trained for."

"But -"

"No, Ev. This is not the time or place for you to test your skills. I know you've been working on your Adrinyn but I can't just allow you to go out when it's this dangerous," he said, putting a hand on her shoulder. There was tenderness in his eyes as he spoke.

"Stay here where it's safe and perhaps there will be something you can help the other Proterezar members with while I'm gone. Besides, Finn has no training and can barely walk and Harris is still recovering from his injuries just like you are." He squeezed her shoulder, leaned over and kissed her cheek and without another word, headed out of the room.

Her face fell and she stopped bouncing excitedly.

"Not the time or place, cogswallop," Eva

muttered under her breath as she scowled at her father's back.

Her ranting continued, turning to walk past me and Harris. "Well, I'm not going to just sit around and be babied by a bunch of old and pretentious has-beens that were -"

"Eva, please," Harris cut in, his deep voice soft but commanding. "We barely made it *here* alive. All three of us are hurt and there is no telling what is going to be out there waiting to pounce."

Her glare shot toward Harris, but he looked at her with earnest. She sighed and her expression softened.

"I *suppose* you're right," she acquiesced. "But hanging out with Elston and Kingsley is the last thing I want to do. Maybe there's something else we could do to help out."

"I vote for sleep," I said, raising a hand, index finger extended. "I don't know about you two, but I'm exhausted. Plus, my nerves are shot. I still have a million questions but I don't know where to begin and I can barely think straight."

Eva and Harris looked at each other and something transpired between them, but nothing was spoken.

"I'll show you to a room. They have cots

here for extended Council meetings when the members might be deadlocked in a discussion or something," Eva offered. "I think I'm going to stay up and try to figure out how to help from here. I've got too much adrenaline to stop moving right now. Besides, the medic advised me to stay awake for some time while the swelling on my head goes down."

"Smart," I said, nodding.

Harris folded his arms across his chest. "I'll stay here and see if the Council members need any help. I'm not really the type to read through a thousand pages of boring Council documents, but I'll see what I can do."

We walked slowly out of the Council chamber and back into the hall with the portraits. The lift downstairs was at the far end of the hall, but we turned back to the corridor that the nurse had brought me down before.

"This must seem unreal to you," Eva offered as we walked. She held onto my arm and allowed me to use her to balance as I walked uneasily down the hallway. It was quiet in the building and there was something peaceful about the stillness.

"Well, in a way, yes. And also, no." I said, tilting my head back and forth as I spoke, weighing the gravity of my situation.

"You see, where I'm from, they have these things called movies. They're like these portraits out here but they move and have sound and people pretend in them and create all sorts of stories that you can watch and be entertained by."

"It sounds similar to our Ocular Projection Mods. You can get an Aug which allows you to see projected images in front of your eye that aren't real but instead is more of an augmented reality scenario you can experience. They're just for fun and mostly just kids are getting them," she said, brushing a stray red hair behind her ear.

"Yeah, sorta. I guess. I don't know, but that sounds pretty cool," I shrugged, continuing my explanation.

"Anyway, in movies, it was really popular for a while for people to pretend that it was the end of the world and various scary creatures were coming out of the ground or a portal from Hell or something and terrorizing the world."

Eva looked perplexed. "Why would anyone want to pretend it was the end of the world? That sounds awful!"

"Well, the world I live in doesn't have the real threat of nightmare creatures coming and overtaking the city and there's a level of excitement and thrill that people seek by going to the movies. They're able to imagine themselves in the scene without real danger and mostly people go to just be scared for a few hours and then move on with their lives. It's an adrenaline junkie kind of thing."

"Oh I see..." Eva's voice trailed off as she chewed on her lip.

"I used to enjoy those movies when I was younger. Going with my friends and seeing who would get the most scared and then trying to freak each other out on the way home was always a lot of fun.

"Now, though, this isn't fun," I continued, "This is terrifying. And I have never been as legitimately scared in my life as I was earlier this evening. The Voidkin in the house, the bar, attacking the train and then being literally confronted by a small horde of them? No thank you." I waved my free hand in a gesture wagging my finger. We turned a corner and headed down another long hallway.

"I'm having a hard enough time trying to wrap my head around being here in the first place. I still have no idea how I got here and why I'm here. But then adding the Void to the whole experience has been almost more than I can take. And then to top it off, I somehow miraculously recovered from my injury."

"Oh that's right," she said, her accent seeping through her words. "I forgot to ask how you were really walking."

"The nurse was about to help redo my bandages and freaked out, called in your dad and he and Harris discussed what I *had* looked like and then looked at my back and arm and they're completely healed. Just one big scar left in its wake. And a crapload of soreness."

Eva stopped abruptly and looked at me wide eyed.

"You're *completely healed*?" Her voice was a mixture of astonishment and utter disbelief.

"Yeah," I replied, laughing a little as it came out. "And I have no idea how or why either."

She started a moment longer and her eyes flicked over my body as she turned to continue walking.

"Well, that is definitely a surprise. And a good one at that. Tonight has been really hard and I'm glad *something* good has happened in all of it." Her voice was distant and she picked up her pace slightly.

"We'll be to the quiet room in just a moment. All of the comms are down so if you need me or someone for whatever the reason, you'll have to call from a hardline. There will be one in the room on the wall next to the restroom. Just pick up the receiver and it should connect you to the Council chambers right away. Take all the time you need."

I smiled at her and thanked her and she left me at the door to the quiet room. I turned the knob and pushed open the door. It was dark inside and it took a moment for my eyes to adjust, even though the light in the hallway behind me wasn't all that bright to begin with. There were bunk bed style cots lining the walls of the room. Nestled in metal frames and wooden borders, the beds looked relatively comfortable and my guess is that they weren't used all that often. At the end of each cot, a pile of folded blankets and several pillows were available. To the right, a doorway opened into a bathroom area with sinks and I'm guessing a toilet or two somewhere over there. The room itself wasn't very large and it had the same feel that everything else did that I'd seen so far - there was a level of antiquity tempered with a refreshing newness as well.

I shuffled over to one of the nearest cots and

tumbled into the bed. I landed on my back and winced as a dull ache rippled through my muscles. Oops. Yeah forgot about that. It's kind of surprising how quickly when you recover from something that the pain and sensitivity you have subsides. You know when you have a sore throat and all you can think about is that pain and every swallow is an experience in torture? Two days later, you are over it and you completely forgot that swallowing was anything different than normal. It's surprising to me that our bodies work that way and it's pretty awesome.

I leaned down, grabbed a pillow and a blanket and got settled to get some much needed rest. My head barely hit the pillow before I fell fast asleep.

CHAPTER EIGHTEEN

I awoke and sat up. Looking around there was light everywhere. Beads of white light dotted the floor of the quiet room. The door was shut. It looked like someone had poked holes in the floor and light streamed through from below. The other beds in the room were gone and the walls seemed far away. The beads of light on the floor began to grow. Soon, light covered the entire floor. I placed a foot off the bed and onto the floor. It was warm and I could feel the heat radiating up my leg. I swiveled off the bed and stood up.

"Hello?" I called out. No response.

As soon as I was upright, the bed behind me sank into the light and within a moment the entire room was filled with bright light. I looked around me but there was nothing but light. Left. Right. Up. Down. Nothing but light.

Soon a small bead of red-orange light shone on the floor and started to take shape. It spread in twists and curves and carved beautiful ornate designs with the light. I stood staring at the growing forms of the red-orange light, mesmerized by its beauty and intricate design. Several moments passed and the basic contours of the room took shape again as the colored light swiveled around the walls and ceiling of the room, encasing me in a beautiful box of red-orange glow, intermingled with the bright white light of the room.

The light pulsed and warmed the entire room comfortably. My skin felt warm and something stirred inside me. I throbbed for more of the warmth and more of the serenity.

Then, I saw a black bead rip from the red-orange light and dance across the room. It swirled around the room and shot in front of my face into the wall nearest to me. The black bead embedded itself in the curved patterns of the colored light, and soon the colored light began to fade to darkness.

The darkness spread quickly and the red-orange light receded. The beautiful patterns of light became dark tendrils, painting across the walls, ceiling and floor. The black seeped from the patterns and infected the white light of the room as well. An inky blackness began dripping from all sides and started to pour over the entire room and over me. I tried moving and getting out of the way, but there was nowhere to turn. The black ooze dripped and spread like a tidal wave and soon there was nothing but black, save for the one square of red-orange light I was standing on.

Soon, all I could see was the blackness in front of me and it started to take shape. From the oozing darkness a huge face started to fill the room. It grew larger and larger beyond what I thought the room could hold. It towered above me and it dripped and splattered fresh inky darkness around the room as it grew.

Finally, the face turned and looked down at me and I felt my breath catch in my throat. I wanted to scream and run as far away as I could but my legs wouldn't move and my voice was gone. I tried again and again in vain but the inky blackness held my feet to the floor. The red-orange light was all but gone by now and the warmth I had felt was swallowed by a pressing cold that threatened to chill my very bones.

The hideous oozing face in front of me

opened it's gigantic mouth and another, smaller form appeared inside. A man, with features pale and starkly contrasted against the pervasive darkness, smiled a yellow, toothy grin and licked his lips. The flesh decayed for a moment and then settled again into pale, veiny colors. The man leaned forward and held out a hand. I couldn't tell if he wanted me to take hold or if he wanted something from me.

I pulled against the ooze holding me there and tried with all my might to get as far away as possible but it was no use. I was completely locked in place, tar like darkness holding me just out of arm's reach of this ghoul.

The man took a step forward, the ooze still dripping all around him from the hideous monster-face rising out of the darkness and he relaxed his arm for a moment. Then, without warning, his smile turned to a snarl and he thrust his hand at my chest and I felt a white-hot pain as his fingers impaled me.

I woke with a gasp.

I looked around, heaving in breaths and clutching a hand to my robe. The quiet room was silent and everything looked the same as it had when I went to sleep. It took several minutes for my heartbeat to calm down and to realize it was only a dream.

You really are going mad, Finn. Tell me about it. I think this entire night has gotten to me. I can't wait for Giles to get back and this to be all over.

Just then, searing pain erupted across my chest. I let out a yelp and pulled open the robe to look down at my skin. There was a small black mark on my chest, right above my heart. It looked like a small cog with a skull face in the center. I rubbed at it, trying to get it to come off but it didn't even smudge.

"What the...?" I muttered. I rubbed the mark and it was tender, but the pain wasn't as fierce now. My muscles ached all over and I had a headache threatening to pound a hole in the back of my head to get out.

There was no way I was going to go back to sleep now, not with my nightmares becoming a reality, so I sat up all the way and swung my legs over the side of the bed. It took a moment for my vision to stop swirling and to push past the throbbing in my head but after a moment, I pushed myself to my feet and shuffled over to the phone on the wall. I don't know what *they* call it but seriously, it was just a phone. It looked like a really really old phone, the kind where its a wooden box and a small earpiece resting on the side and a horn in the center to speak into. The wooden box was, unsurprisingly, ornate and there was metal laced throughout its design as well.

Man, these people love their wood and metal designs.

I picked up the earpiece and then leaned into the mouthpiece and started speaking.

"Hello? Eva? Council members? Anyone getting this?"

Silence.

I tapped on the little piece that the receiver had been hanging on and tried again.

"Can anyone hear me?"

Silence.

"Well, this was useless." I said. As I went to put the earpiece back on the stand, I heard something through the phone. It sounded like someone breathing really heavily on the other end.

"Hello?" I asked

Again, only breathing

"Eva? Elston? Harris? Is that you?"

Breathing.

I let it go on for another moment and then decided to just go back down the hall to see what they were doing.

Before I could hang up, however, a voice on the other end began speaking in low, guttural tones and seemed like it struggled to form words.

"We will find you, Finnegan Riley." And the line then went dead.

My heart sank in my chest and I swallowed hard. I threw the receiver back on the stand and started to panic. I ran to the door from the hallway, cracked it open and peered out. All of the lights lining the hallway before were barely on, and most of them were flickering. The hall itself was empty but I got the feeling that it wasn't going to be that way for long. I shut the door, locked it and then searched the room for something to secure the door. There was a metal chair sitting in the corner next to a small work desk. I dashed over, grabbed it and jammed it under the knob of the door in hopes that it might slow down whatever was coming to get me.

My mind raced. *Think Finn, think. How can I get out of this room and find some place safe? Is there anyplace safe anymore? I thought they couldn't get into here! It doesn't matter. Just get out of here. Is there a window or anything I could go out? But they can fly. And I sure as heck can't. And we're something like 82 stories up in the sky. And even that might not be right. I don't know, I don't know, I don't know.*

I scanned the room for anywhere I might be able to escape. The only exit from this room was the door I had just barred and the small windows periodically dotting the walls.

I went to the bathroom at the back of the room and searched in there for anywhere I might be able to hide or escape. There were several shower stalls and a few water closets. There were no readily accessible vents or ducts I could shimmy into. See, now, if this were the movies, there would magically be some duct that I could wrestle my way into in just the knick of time. Then again, in the movies, the monster is always waiting for the hero in the duct, too.

I ran back out to the other room and to find something I could use to protect myself but I was quickly running out of options. There was nothing I could wield as an improvised weapon. Not even a table lamp I could grab. Just a bunch of beds and pillows and sheets.

At once, an idea formed in my mind. It wasn't a great idea, but it was something.

I dashed around the room, throwing the pillows on the beds and aligning them like they were people sleeping. I hastily threw the blankets overtop and tousled the pillows to look like sleeping people under their covers. After about a minute, it looked roughly like there were fifteen or so people sleeping in their beds and I hoped the Voidkin weren't the savviest of creatures. All I needed was for it to buy me a few moments.

I pulled the metal chair out from under the door knob. I took it back to the desk behind the door and then crawled under the desk, pulling the chair in front of me and waited.

Man, if I thought that my heart had pounded earlier this evening, I'm pretty sure I was giving my blood pressure a run for its money. I was going to need to get some sort of medication if I had to keep this up.

I waited in silence. The room was completely quiet. There was no motion out in the hallway and the faint humming from the lights in the hall lamps was all that I could hear. It seemed like an eternity passed as I sat there, crunched up underneath the small metal desk and waited for the inevitable entrance of a Voidkin.

Minutes passed. I tried to keep myself calm

and just focus on breathing so as to be ready for action once the creature was inside the room.

Several more minutes passed. I held onto the legs of the chair in front of me and I could tell that my hands were getting tired and cramping up a little bit. I decided to let go of the chair and wait until the door swung open to enact my plan. All I needed to do was get out of this room. Once I was out of the room, I could run for help and it could be a fair fight. Or, well, maybe a *more* fair fight. Me trapped in a room with nothing to defend myself is definitely *not* fair.

It felt as though time moved at a snail's pace and I wanted to scream in frustration. I was a ball of energy and nerves and something needed to give or I was going to burst.

Another minute ticked by and I strained to listen, trying to hear activity in the hallway. Just then, I heard it. A faint 'click-clack' of shoes on the marble tile. I threw my hands up to grab the chair and readied myself. I had one shot at getting this right or I was dead. Or worse.

I shuddered at the thought and focused in on the door. *Focus Finn. You just have to make it out the door. Wait until it is investigating the beds and then make a break for it.*

The sound in the hallway grew louder until it was right outside the door. The knob turned and the door pushed open. I held my breath and my muscles tensed as I readied to push the chair and run for the door.

"Finn?" A young man's voice quietly called into the room.

I paused, hands still tight on the legs of the chair, knuckles white with tension.

"Finn, are you still sleeping?" Harris called again.

The tension in my body relaxed. It was Harris coming to check on me. Man am I on edge or *what!*

I quietly pushed the chair out from in front of me and scrambled to my feet. Harris stepped in the door and waited a moment for his eyes to adjust. That was just long enough for me to move over to him and not look like I had been cowering under a desk.

He looked around the room and confusion swept over his face.

"Who messed up all the beds?" he asked, turning to me.

"Don't worry about it," I offered, "I'll put them all back in a little bit." My heart was still pounding and beads of sweat had dotted my forehead. I took a deep breath and tried to look casual.

"Hey, so, uhh, I came to get you. It's been a few hours and we haven't heard from any of the Council teams that went out yet. Eva has a plan, but I didn't want to just leave you here without notice."

"Oh, thanks," I said, rubbing the back of my neck and smiling.

"It looks like you were up already. Why didn't you call down to us?" Harris asked, still looking around the room.

Warning lights started going off in my head. My eyes went wide and I stopped moving.

"What do you mean? I tried calling down to you."

"No," Harris said, "the landline hasn't gone off at all. I just told you no one has called in yet and we're getting worried."

"Well, *I'm* telling you I tried. I went over and picked up the receiver and tried getting ahold of you guys."

"Show me," he said, gesturing to the phone on the wall.

I repeated the same steps as before. This

time, though, Eva's voice came through the earpiece, clear as day.

"Hey you! Thought you were going to sleep the night away." Her voice was surprisingly bright and energized considering how long she had been up at this point.

"Look, we need to discuss some things," she said. "The teams haven't checked in yet and -"

"Yeah, Harris is here. He told me. We'll be right down."

The line went still for a moment. When she spoke again, Eva's voice was completely different. The energy was still there but her tone was serious and direct.

"Finn, Harris hasn't left the room. He's standing next to me."

My throat went dry and I glanced over at the young man standing next to me.

"Oh really?" I said, trying my best to keep my voice even. "Well, you know how I get lost so it'll be nice to have someone escort me back." I emphasized the words.

"We'll be right there Finn." Eva said urgently. I heard the click of the call ending and my whole body started to tense up once again.

"Alright then, let's get going!" the guy in

front of me said.

"After you!" I replied, gesturing to the door.

At this, his entire demeanor shifted and his face darkened, but the smirk never left his lips.

"Oh, no. Please. After you." His words dripped like poisoned honey, lazily slipping from his lips with a cool edge. "You're *injured* after all."

As he spoke, his eyes flashed a bright red and he touched his tongue to his lip.

I wasted no time. I booked it for the door, throwing the chair behind me as I ran. The creature lunged at me and barely missed as I skirted past him. He got tangled in the chair and I made a fast break for the door. I flung it wide open and took the corner at the top speed I could muster.

I heard a deep unintelligible muttering behind me and *felt* the darkness reach out for me. A moment later, a stabbing pain ripped through my chest and I nearly collapsed. The spot where that mark had appeared during my dream was searing hot and felt like it was burning a hole all the way through me to my back. I took in a sharp breath but continued running.

In a flash, the man appeared directly in front of me and I pulled up short. He no longer looked like Harris but instead the horrifying pale man I had seen outside the elevator hours before. He may have been a head shorter than the Voidkin, but he was still a massive creature and had a good six inches on me, and I'm already pretty tall. He reached out and grabbed me by the robe and yanked me in close to his face.

"I don't like being interrupted," he snarled. His breath was acrid and he gave off a stench that smelled like rotten flesh and of death itself.

"Well, I'm sorry, but I don't like being killed!" I shot back. Not my wittiest retort, but hey, I was panicking.

His lips curled into a smile and his yellowing teeth peeked out between those horrific lips of his.

"Just tell me where the shard is, Finn. Then, you can just go back to a normal, simple life back home."

"I don't know what you're talking about. And I'm pretty sure that even if I did, I wouldn't be sharing with the likes of you."

"Oh, you're a bold one, aren't you?" the creature said.

He put a finger on my chest with his free hand and the white hot searing pain ripped through me once again. I let out a scream and kicked at him, trying to break free. The blows glanced off his body and he didn't even flinch. I kept trying to wrestle from his grip while stealing a glance around to try and see if anything near me could help. As I struggled, something caught my eye behind him.

"Last time asking nicely, Finnegan. Where. Is. The. Shard!?" He punctuated every word with venomous accents. His voice was cold but sophisticated. It made the entire experience all the more terrifying, I think. There is something wholly unnerving about someone so polite being calculating about how they're going to rip you apart with their bare hands. As he spoke, spittle flew from his mouth and landed on my face and neck.

"Well, since you asked so nicely, I'll just tell you then," I replied sarcastically, and squeezed shut my eyes.

From behind him, a flash of light tore through the hallway and a force knocked both of us to the ground. The Felmaven toppled next to me and I ended up dazed on the ground. Without missing a beat, the creature was on its feet again, writhing in a mass of darkness. Instantly, his form changed as the vaguely humanoid man was towering in the hallway, looking like a wraith with strips of darkness casting off behind it. It zigzagged down the hallway and lunged at Kingsley. The frail little man in his obnoxious blue suit pivoted and the Felmaven sailed past him. Elston, arm still outstretched with a god-honest freaking *wand* in his hand turned and flicked his wrist again. This time, the flash of light was more contained and both heat and force rippled down the hallway. The Felmaven buckled and vanished in a puff of darkness.

Elston dropped his hand to his side and turned to meet my gaze. Kingsley, standing behind him off to his left, had a small pistol in his hand, obscured somewhat by the cuff of his oversized jacket. Percipity stood there looking ready for bear with a pretty slick looking katana in her hands, a ripple of purple electricity casting down its blade. Behind them, Harris and Eva stood poised, ready for action.

"He isn't gone. Stay alert," Elston snapped, speaking over his shoulder to the crew with him.

"Get up boy," the gaunt Ekori said, beckoning toward me. I scrambled to my feet and hustled as best I could over to them. The six of us stood in a small cluster and guarded ourselves against any further attack.

After a moment, a draught of black smoke appeared again at the end of the hallway and the Felmaven materialized, dark tendrils of black ooze surrounding him. Kingsley raised his pistol and took aim at the figure. The pistol was similar to the one I had seen with Lydia earlier, formed completely of gears and sprockets and a see-through barrel with a small bead of electricity zipping back and forth through the opening. Kingsley pulled the trigger and a bubble of electricity sailed down the hallway to where the Felmaven stood.

A smile touched the creatures lips again as if this was some sort of a game and he disappeared, reappearing again closer to us and the electric charge behind him. The Felmaven's eyes flashed red and with a wave of his hand sent several oozing tentacles and grabbed at Elston and Percipity.

The Council members reacted in a flurry of motion. Percipity slashed her katana in one fluid arch, severing the black tentacles from their source. Elston raised his wand and muttered something I couldn't understand and an azure beam sailed down the hallway directly at the creature.

The Felmaven pulled up a hand in front of its chest and a wall of black appeared, absorbing the beam. As it dissipated, the creature threw both hands out in front of it and more tendrils swarmed toward us. Simultaneously, crackles of thin red lightning charged from his outstretched hands and sunk deep into Elston and Percipity. They were stunned momentarily and the tendrils swerved to encase them.

Pinned, the two Council members wrestled against the tentacles. Kingsley broke into a cockeyed grin and flipped open a latch on his gun. He pushed a button and the bubble of electricity down the hall detonated, filling the corridor with a sonic blast behind the Felmaven. The creatures eyes grew wide as it was blasted forward, the darkness surrounding it obliterated by the wave. The tendrils encasing the other Council members vaporized and the two were free once again. The Felmaven pushed himself up, his face etched in a snarl and dashed into the quietroom once again.

A moment later there was the sound of breaking glass. We hustled toward the room to check, the three Ekori leading the way. Sure enough, the room was empty, save for a broken window which the Felmaven had apparently jumped through.

Elston turned to the other Council members

and spoke in rapid succession to each.

"Percipity, secure the room. Make sure that the Felmaven or any other Voidkin are unable to return this way. Kingsley, head down the hall to the back entry for the enclave and see how the Felmaven made his way in here. Once you know, do your best to secure it or send for reinforcements. My guess is that the security teams on the other end are either dead or didn't know that it was a Felmaven. If he was truly disguised as Mr. Archer, it would be nearly impossible to tell. I will ensure these three are escorted safely back to the Proterezar chambers. Once you are through, reconvene on our location. We have some decisions to make."

The other Council members nodded once and without a word, headed to their tasks. Elston turned to us, and strode past without giving us a second glance. His pace was brisk and it was hard for me to keep up. Thankfully, Eva and Harris helped me along and movement got easier every passing minute.

We arrived back at the Council chamber and the guards nodded to the Ekorius and opened the door for him. Ekorius Blackwell stopped and spoke to the guards for a brief moment.

"Double check security on *anyone* entering the complex. There has been an attack, which you likely just heard the result of. The creature attempting to infiltrate was assuming the appearance of one of our young guests here and could very well try again."

"Yes sir," the guards replied in unison.

Elston brushed past them, his jacket tails billowing out behind him as he walked. We followed him into the chamber and the large metal doors closed behind us.

As soon as they were shut, Elston turned on his heel and got within about two inches of my face.

"*Why* are they after you, boy?" he demanded, his voice stern and abrupt. He had a finger raised toward my chin and was very clearly trying to intimidate me.

You see, here's the thing about me. When someone wants to intimidate me, I'm much less inclined to comply. I was bullied a lot as a kid and I learned pretty early on that the easiest way to take the wind from their sails was simply to not give in. So I checked my attitude and stared disinterestedly at him as he fumed. Add to that the fact that he and I were about the same height, and I wasn't about to give in to this belligerent old man.

"Look, I have no idea what is going on here and I have no idea why they keep coming after me," I said, tone even and staring through Elston.

"I appreciate that you came and saved me, along with the other Council members. There was no way I was getting out of that alive if you guys hadn't come along when you did. But I don't know why they want me, aside from the fact that the creepy old guy keeps asking me about a shard." I took a step back and tried to diffuse the tension by giving Blackwell some space.

I continued, "I have no idea what shard they're talking about and I'm not about to give him anything even if I did have it. But I don't. And I don't know what it is." I kept going, pushing the point. "Are you getting the fact that *I don't know what is going on!*"

Elston put his hand down and took a moment to straighten his waistcoat and compose himself.

"Yes, well..." His voice trailed off as he fumbled with what to say next.

Eva broke into the conversation, putting a hand on my chest and a hand outstretched to the Ekorius.

"Look, gentlemen, please. Ekorius Blackwell, Finn is telling you the truth. He really has no idea what is happening right now and is probably not going to be able to shed light on the events of the evening, aside from being attacked several times by agents of the Void." Her tone was placating but carried an air of authority with it.

"We need to establish how the Felmaven even got in here and the other Council members are already on that. We also need to figure out why no one has checked in yet and what has happened to my father." Ekorius Blackwell gave a little "humph" and turned to go back to his chair at the boardroom table. Eva turned and looked at me, blue eyes pleading to 'play nice.' I nodded at her and the three of us walked to the table as well.

Eva sat down and surveyed all the papers in front of her. Sighing heavily, she rubbed at her temples, tilted her head to each side, stretching her neck and then seemed ready to dig in.

I walked over and sat down beside her. Harris and Blackwell joined as well. A few moments passed before anyone spoke again.

"So what do we know?" I said finally, breaking the silence.

Eva turned to me, her soft voice quivering.

"Nothing. We know nothing. Last we heard from the teams was when they left our facility. No one has checked in. I'm beginning to get really worried."

She absentmindedly chewed on her thumbnail and looked up at me worriedly. I put a reassuring hand on her shoulder but didn't know what to say.

Blackwell spoke up, clearing his throat. "Yes, well. It is highly unlikely that they are in any imminent danger, though it is surprising that none of them have checked in whatsoever."

To me, his voice sounded like a mouse getting pressed slowly through a cheese grater. The only retort I could come up with was "thanks captain obvious" but that seemed petty. I changed approach.

"Have we double checked to make sure that the landlines are working?" I offered. "I mean, I even had a problem calling down to you guys from the quiet room earlier."

The three of them abruptly turned to look at me.

I shrugged. "Yeah, the first time I picked up the phone," I gestured to the device on the wall near us, "it sounded like dead air, except for heavy breathing. Then a creepy voice came on and told me they were going to find me. Clearly, they were right." A shudder slid down my back and I felt uneasy just thinking about it.

"The only time we heard from you was when we realized you were in danger," Eva said.

"Well, I *did* try it twice. But the first time apparently the Void had tapped into it or something." I said.

"We'd best check the lines, then!" Elston chimed in, his shrill voice causing me to twitch slightly as he scrambled to the landline on the wall across the table from him. "If you experienced some sort of interference, then it's entirely possible that the teams are experiencing that as well. Maybe the Void has wormed its way into our system and has command of our communications."

Just then, the large metal doors slid open and Percipity and Kingsley both walked back into the Council chamber.

"All of the rooms are secure and we should be safe for the time being," Percipity offered, unhooking the sheath of her katana from her waist and walking toward the table with it in hand.

"And the guards on the far end are also safe. They've been alerted to the situation and will be taking exceptional measures in admitting anyone to our level. I also took the liberty of stationing a double post on both ends," Kingsley said, his voice upbeat and full of life.

"Superb," Elston agreed, shifting back to the conversation at the table.

"We've established that the Void may have wormed into our communications at the very core of the hardwired landlines. It will take a few minutes to examine things on our end so let's not jump to any conclusions until we diagnose our situation here," he said, gesturing to Kingsley and escorting the shorter man to the phone on the wall.

The two men managed to get the casing off the wall without issue and set to investigating the wires and the inner workings of the contraption. From my vantage, I couldn't really see what was going on, but there were occasional sparks and flare ups and I was sure that one or both of them were using their Adrinyn to figure things out.

As they worked, Harris dragged his chair over closer to me and Eva.

"So, if we don't hear from the teams...?" he asked, letting the question hang in the air.

"I don't know," Eva replied. "I can't stand the thought of leaving my dad out in the darkness.

I'd want to go find him. Or at least be able to locate him and send help."

"At this point, this place doesn't seem any safer to me than the outside did." I added, gesturing around me. "Terrifying creatures posing as people I know? How did he even do that?"

"No idea," Eva replied frankly, half heartedly shuffling through papers . "Felmaven were somewhat of a myth up until a few hours ago when you met one. If we all hadn't been there to see it too, I'm not sure anyone would've believed you earlier. I mean, I can understand where Blackwell is coming from, but he can't deny that fact even now. I'm sure he's a bit rattled like the rest of us, even though he'd never admit it. He's a stubborn old man." She periodically glanced over at the men working on the landline as she spoke.

"Great," I offered in exasperation. "I barely knew you guys two days ago, but over the last day, I felt like I at least had someone I could trust. Now I feel like I can't trust my own senses."

"Maybe we should come up with a code word?" Harris offered.

"Given the circumstances, I think that's actually a pretty smart idea," I said, nodding to Harris.

"Let's use something so obscure no one would actually think of it!" he said, excitement gathering in his voice.

"I know, let's say, 'the Hemshult gives the Turnblad a Jillywoppen,' " Harris continued.

Eva and I looked at each other, then at Harris. If question marks could have literally floated above my head, I believe that they would have.

"Or what if we just said 'The Raven' and you reply 'flies at night.' Then we both have to say something and we don't have to memorize crazy talk," Eva said, one eyebrow still raised toward Harris.

Harris' shoulders drooped a bit at being shot down, but he nodded. "Yeah, I suppose that works too."

Eva and I smiled at him. He looked really young right now and it was fun to see him so excited over something so trivial. Sometimes all of us need to let our inner kid out more often. I'm guessing Harris liked to pretend he was a spy back when he was a kid and he was finally getting the chance to live some of that out. I bet he wishes it was under better circumstances.

"I'm not waiting around here much longer. I

may not be 'council level' status in my Adrinyn ability but I can fend for myself out there," Eva said.

I wasn't convinced. She was feisty and doggedly loyal, I'd give her that much. But we'd already tangled with the Voidkin on multiple occasions and I didn't see her using any sort of tech style magic. The Voidkin were seriously nothing to shake a stick at. Even worse, the Felmaven was still out there, and it had given three Ekori a run for their money. Supposedly, they were the top of the top when it came to using those skills.

Just then, a small flash and crackle came from the duo working on the landline and Kingsley yelped. He held one hand clutched in the other and was hopping from one foot to the other.

"I believe we got it!" Blackwell said.

"Except for my hand!" Kingsley said through clenched teeth.

Ekorius Blackwell replaced the casing and picked up the receiver to listen. We all turned to look, hoping that they'd gotten it all fixed.

Kingsley, still bouncing up and down spoke up as Elston listened in the phone. "There was definitely something blocking our communication to outside sources. They were using a Scarab device to burrow into our end and block any incoming and outgoing communication. Hopefully we got it fixed and we'll be able to make contact now -"

As Kingsley spoke, Elston's face grew long and his eyes darkened. He grabbed Kingsley by the shoulder and squeezed, and abruptly the little man ceased speaking.

Elston set down the receiver on the small table attached to the phone casing and lifted his wand to it. Instantly, the sound from the earpiece was magnified and filled the entire room.

Giles' voice came through in broken static.

"...Couldn't   stop   it.....you......the ritual.....before we got he.......need help."

It was difficult to figure out exactly what he was saying. Sounds of terrifying roars and screams littered the background behind his voice, punctuated by the occasional crack of a whip. The next part of the message came through more clearly, though.

"...Ambushed...August and Lydia are down...I can't hold them off much longer...please reply, Cogspit!"

An explosion sounded in the background and the line went dead.

CHAPTER NINETEEN

I felt the blood drain from my face. Everyone in the room was stunned. No one spoke for a long minute.

"We have to go help them," Eva said, breaking the silence. Her voice was quiet and choked, a whisper.

"We have to," she said again, clearing her throat and forcing confidence into her voice. She gathered her coat and stood to her feet, wasting no time.

"Eva, wait," Percipity called out. "We don't even know how long ago that was. They could have sent that message an hour ago. There is no telling what could be waiting for us out there."

Eva spun on her heel and glared at the taller

woman. "My *father* is out there, possibly dying. He is the *only* family I have left and by the Ember, if you so much as try and stop me I will put up a fight like you've never seen." I could see the tears forming in her eyes.

Percipity's face softened, her rich voice soothing. "No, Eva. I'm not going to stop you. I don't want to see your father harmed any more than I do the others with him. I just don't want you to go alone and without someone to help keep you safe."

The tall Ekorius stood and picked up the sheath holding her katana and clipped it onto her back.

"Ekori Elston and Kingsley," Percipity said, turning to the two older gentlemen, "I will accompany young Ms. Fleming to the Thornsby estate. If you are able to restore any more of the communications, I will make sure we check in each opportunity we come across a landline throughout the city."

"We're joining you," I chimed in. "If someone has a spare weapon or something, I'm sure I could be of some use."

Harris nodded and echoed my sentiments and we moved to join the ladies. Eva smiled a small, thankful smile but her face was set and I could tell she was mentally preparing for the worst.

Eva pulled together her outfit. I hadn't really noticed until now, but she had changed at some point since we arrived in the Council area, probably while I was 'sleeping.' Her dark brown pants had been exchanged for black pants and high laced combat boots. On top, she was sporting a forest green tank-top of sorts, covered by a thick black wool coat that cast down to her ankles. I'm not sure how or when she managed to scrounge one up, but she was also wearing a shoulder holster, equipped with one of those small handguns with the electricity crackling through it and was busy tightening the leather strap across her chest.

It took a second for me to notice, but as I watched Eva gear up, Kingsley appeared at my side, holding out a similar looking gun to the one he was using earlier. I glanced down at it and nodded in affirmation. I took hold of the grip and hefted the gun from his hands.

I've used guns before in my life, but never in anything more than a recreational experience. My buddies and I spent a few afternoons at the shooting range and I even had the chance to go skeet shooting with shotguns at an Olympic size shooting range, but I wouldn't say that I was a pro at using a firearm. Given what I'd seen of these particular weapons, I felt doubly sure I had no idea what I was doing.

Kingsley must have sensed my discomfort. He spoke up, voice clipped and informational, not at all the chipper, somewhat crazy I'd come to expect at this point.

"Now, if you're going to go with them and not end up killing yourself or any of them, here are a few pointers. First, ensure that the safety is on until you are in a hot situation." He motioned to a small lever on the side of the barrel. He switched it once to the "off" position and then back "on" to show me.

"Second," he continued, "in the event you do need to fire on a Voidkin or some such, note that this particular weapon isn't going to stop a monstrosity barreling down on you. It is designed more for suppressive fire or to take out targets at medium range if your accuracy is spot on. Always aim for the head if you're able, but don't sacrifice a hit for the sake of a kill. Sometimes, wounding is as useful as killing.

"Third, ammunition. This photon pistol discharges bolts of particalized energy which will disrupt the electromagnetic field of whatever you hit, which is typically enough to stun a person in addition to wounding them. Voidkin are significantly larger than normal humans, so it'll probably take a few extra shots to bring them down. Once they're down, though, they won't be getting back up.

"Speaking of a few extra shots, the ammunition is stored in these small containers and has a set number of charges." He handed me several vials of what looked like blue curacao. There was only a small bit of room in the vial aside from the liquid, but as I rotated the vial, the liquid moved and revealed small metal prongs on either end inside of the vial. I glanced back at the pistol in my hands and took note that the barrel of the gun housed the blue vial, with only a small muzzle on one end and the body of the gun on the other. An electric charge ran through the blue liquid on the gun.

Kingsley continued, "If you need to reload, simply press this mechanism and it'll discharge the empty canister." He pushed a clasp at the end of the barrel and the vial currently loaded in the gun clicked slightly out of place. The electricity flowing through the liquid immediately ceased and the vial darkened. He pulled the vial out and held it up for me to see and continued speaking.

"Then just replace the vial, grip-end first and you're set. Shouldn't take more than a moment. Just pay attention to the level of transformer fluid you have left and you shouldn't run into any problems." He clicked the same vial back into place and the liquid lit up once again, electricity zipping between the sets of metal prongs.

"Finally," he added, turning the gun over in my hand, "if you get into real hot water, you can set the charger to overload and use the weapon itself as an improvised explosive." He motioned to a set of two buttons on the grip near to the chamber.

"If you press these two simultaneously for four seconds, you'll see the charge in the barrel begin to light up brighter than normal and you'll have roughly four more seconds to toss it before it detonates. If you go this route, make sure you throw it a good distance and still duck for cover. The blast is determined by the remaining amount of transformer fluid left in your current canister. Obviously, the more fluid you have, the larger the blast. The average blast radius of the detonation is about 15 meters, if you have used up several shots. So that means you could take out a decent size squad of goons on your tail if need be. That radius could grow or shrink depending on if it is a full or almost empty canister, but that's the average. Either way, be careful and find cover if you choose to detonate the charge. But remember, that'll leave you unarmed and so should really only be a last resort."

"Thanks Kingsley," I said, shaking his hand. "This will help immensely. Speaking of finding cover and protection, I'd better find some real clothing and get ready to go."

He bobbed his head up and down, his wild hair flopping crazily about him then simply turned and walked away.

Harris took me to a room just outside the Council chambers to find a change of clothes. Above the door, a small illuminated sign stated this was "The Depot." The room was small and lockers lined one wall. On the far end, a small arsenal of weaponry waited behind cages guarded with keypads and physical padlocks. A few generic standard issue uniforms were folded and put away in the locker marked "spare uniforms," farthest from the entrance. I grabbed a set and changed quickly. They fit alright but it wasn't a perfect match. It certainly wasn't the comfortability of denim and polyester, either. The only clothes they had for me were a loose fitting linen shirt, a set of the dark heavy combat fatigues and a jacket that the guards on duty throughout the Council area had been wearing. The fatigues itched and were slightly too small for me. The pants in particular were uncomfortably short and rode up very unpleasantly. Being tall and lanky doesn't usually lend itself to easily finding clothes that fit. But, given that we were looking to head back out into a terrifying hellscape of impenetrable darkness, running around in medical robes seemed even *less* practical.

I suited up and returned to the Council chamber. Eva looked up from the table and I'm pretty sure I saw her stifle a laugh as I strode into the room. Percipity either didn't notice or didn't comment because she finished gathering her belongings and headed straight for the door. Harris had also changed from his attire to a similar combat suit, except his fit him perfectly. He was a head shorter than me, but he was significantly better built than I was and the fatigues seemed to accentuate his musculature, making him look even more like he could beat the pulp out of you if you crossed him. He was not, however, wearing the jacket. Instead, he wore a tight fitting, black cloth shirt that had the appearance of being reinforced somehow, a small diamond pattern glinting off the light if you caught it just right. His right arm was exposed and the contraption bracing his arm twisted its way to his shoulder and ornately wove around his arm, with thick stems of metal interlaced around his forearm and wrist with cogs and sprockets at his joints so it could move and gave way to looser strands of metal the higher up it went on his arm. He had two side arms locked into place in opposing shoulder holsters. I'm pretty sure that if I had met him in any other circumstance, I would have worked hard to not cross him.

Eva also looked ridiculously intimidating. She had the gun I saw her holster earlier under her coat, but also had a long staff strapped to her back and another gun in her right hand. Percipity was the only one who didn't change, still dressed in her long golden dress from earlier with her katana fastened across her back and a small device coiled around her ear. She pushed open the Council chamber doors and headed for the lift entrance.

Eva was quick on her heels and Harris beckoned to me and we pulled up the rear. The Proterezar chamber doors closed heavily behind us and we loaded into the elevator, not entirely sure what we would find.

The lift kicked into motion and I piped up, "Does anyone know if we have gotten any contact from any of the other groups yet?"

Percipity's mouth tightened at the edges and she spoke quickly, "No, we haven't, unfortunately. Our first priority is to get to Dr. Fleming and the others and find out what happened at Thornsby's. Then, we'll assess the situation and move on to find the others."

It was silent for the remainder of the ride down from the Proterezar. The air was thick with anticipation and, at least on my part, fear. I wasn't thrilled about going back out to the streets where the Voidkin were roaming. But it wasn't really a matter of preference at this point. From the sound of things, this was going to be the "new normal" if we didn't do something. And I didn't even know what normal was here! So, I wrestled down my fear and put on my game face. If these guys could keep it cool in the face of danger, so could I. Just think Finn, you stared down a mountain lion and lived to tell about it. That should be enough to bolster anyone's confidence.

The lift descended for several minutes. I

wished I could see the city. Fear and adrenaline aside, my curiosity was as active as ever and I wanted to explore this mysterious place. For now, though, there was nothing but pervasive darkness pressed against the glass of the lift.

"I think it would be better if we took the Network and worked our way toward the Rigsturn Ward that way," Percipity said, breaking the silence.

"Sounds good," Eva said, staring blankly ahead. I couldn't tell if she was just really focused or was having second thoughts about this whole expedition.

The Ekorius nodded to Harris and the young man pressed his hand against the control panel. Blue-white sparks leapt from his hand to the console and our descent quickened. We passed the ground floor and continued underground. From what I could see, there were no controls in the cabin of the lift which would've allowed us to simply navigate there by pushing a button. I got the sense that the Network was designed with the intention of being a useful tool for those who could access it, and a mystery to those who could not. Or at least it was not as accessible to everyone.

The lift doors opened and I saw a dimly lit

metal hallway like back at the Dragon's Burrow. Corrugated metal lined the walls and sparse light bulbs hung from wire overhead every fifteen feet or so.

Percipity strode into the hallway first. Eva followed the Ekorius. Harris and I followed behind, allowing the Ekorius Emerson to lead the way. We progressed down the passage and turned left at the first junction. The hall before us stretched on and I was confronted with the thought that this was not going to be a short trip.

"So how far away is the Thornsby estate?" I asked.

The Ekorius replied without looking, her deep voice calm and factual. "Navigating the Network is tricky, but will likely be the most direct route considering the state of the mass transit of the city. We cannot risk trying the Lightrail for fear that we may experience a similar attack that you three endured on your way out of Etherborough. We also do not have a guarantee that there aren't other unused units on the track and it would be a suicide mission to go that way."

"Right...but *how far away* is the Thornsby estate?" I asked, unable to mask my sarcastic jab.

Percipity shot me a glance and then her

expression smoothed. "If we are fortunate and don't run into any snags along the way, we should be able to make it just over an hour."

"We're lucky it isn't Etherborough or Caperhallow," Harris added. "Those would probably take us days to navigate.

"Indeed, that would be quite unfortunate," Percipity offered.

I nodded my thanks and allowed the silence to once again fall on our group.

I just couldn't get a handle on the Councilwoman. On the one hand, she was direct and polite. On the other, she was this calculating menace who looked legitimately terrifying with her katana and fancy dress. But the pitch of her voice never wavered or betrayed much emotion whatsoever. If I didn't know better, I'd say she was an impressive killer robot instead of simply a well-spoken, composed woman. Although now that I think about it, I *don't* know better. In the span of the past day or so, I had learned that there was such a thing as magic, although they didn't call it that, and humans can manipulate electronics with the sheer power of their will and there is some sort of portal contraption that can yank you from one dimension to another and there are literal, *real* manifestations of evil out there. Who's to say they didn't also have really awesome killer robot women, too?

We traveled in silence. We worked our way down slender metal hallways and turned the corner each time to be greeted by the same exact view: metal walls and Edison bulbs. How any of them had any idea where they were going was beyond me. There were no distinguishing marks on the walls or any sort of indicators that would let the weary traveler know they were going the correct direction.

"So how do you know where to go?" I asked, my curiosity breaking the silence.

"The Network is a blessing and a curse to our great city. It is mostly used by the Proterezar and those on official city business, though there are sections where a few of the more seasoned residents of the districts above have managed to figure out the complex passageways," the Ekorius offered.

"It is not an easy place to navigate," she continued, "but it gives unabridged access to most areas of the entire city. You could travel from one end of Emberwall to the other without ever having to access the surface. That kind of unrestricted access comes with a cost." As she spoke, the councilwoman adjusted the strap holding her sword to a more comfortable position.

"The cost of that access is knowledge. As it is with many things in the world, those who have the knowledge hold genuine power. Brute force is always something to be reckoned with, but knowledge is the true key to any amount of power. And so in ages past, a previous Proterezar Council deemed that the Emberwall citizens are free to wander the Network if they so choose, but it would be at their own peril. It is entirely possible to get lost without any sense of direction and never find a way back out."

"That seems intense," I said. "Can't everyone just get to the other areas of the city on the transit system? Or on foot on the roads?"

"Not necessarily." Eva chimed in, looking over her shoulder at me. "There are areas of Emberwall which are completely restricted from the general public, like Blackfort. It occupies several levels of Netherward and all access is restricted from anyone going there unless you work there. Everyone else has to take a different shuttle and it adds a fairly significant delay to those attempting to get around the Netherward. Well, it adds a few minutes to anyone's commute but still, that can get frustrating at times."

"There are other areas that are completely off limits too, but you should know that by now young man," Percipity added, not turning her head to look, her voice even and unreadable.

Right. Forgot that the rest of the Council doesn't know about my *unique* circumstances. I wonder why Kingsley bothered to explain the ins and outs of the gun to me in that case. Maybe I just look really dumb or something. Or perhaps he was being overly helpful. Yeah, I'll go with that one.

"Right, well it's great to have someone so knowledgeable with us to help guide us!" I said, trying to sound like I knew what I was doing. I didn't.

The Ekorius continued leading our group down different corridors, turning left or right, opening and closing doors behind us with no real observable pattern. Every once in a while, she would take a small round disk out of her pocket and fasten it to the wall after a turn or entering a door. She was rather sly about the whole thing too. It took me a while of watching to notice her doing anything at all.

After roughly fifteen minutes, we came upon

a small box in the center of the passage we were walking down and Percipity stopped.

"Wait a moment," she said, putting a hand to the box and feeling around the edges. A second later, the metal box popped off the wall and revealed a smaller, wooden box phone similar to the one up in the Proterezar. This one wasn't as fancy, but seemed to operate similarly. It was dusty and evidently had not been used for some time. The Ekorius picked up the ear piece and held it to her ear. There were several cogs interlaced on the front of the wooden box, all with alternating larger and smaller sprockets. Percipity twisted several of them in different directions until the larger sprockets were facing toward each other. Then she waited.

Several long moments passed as she stood there, holding up the ear piece and listening. It felt as though we were waiting forever, when her face fell slightly and she replaced the receiver on the hook along the side of the wooden box.

"No response from Central," she said, her tone even and cool as always. "I imagine they're still working on examining the extent of the damage to the communications system and the Network is likely low on the priority list. We know they've extracted the Scarab from the Thornsby estate, so we should continue on and attempt communication once again from there."

She replaced the metal box with a satisfying click as it lodged back into place over the phone on the wall. The Ekorius turned and continued walking as if nothing serious was happening.

"How are you so calm right now?" I asked.

"What do you mean?" The taller woman asked, still not making eye contact and pressing forward without looking back at me.

"Well, today has been a whirlwind of adventure for me with the whole 'almost getting killed a couple of times by Voidkin' thing. You are just so even-keeled and it's like nothing ruffles your feathers."

"An odd analogy," she replied, eyes scanning the hallway ahead of us.

"But there is always a logical reason for what is going on and no reason for that to disturb our sensibilities. We have a task to accomplish and it is least helpful to allow mundane inconsistencies to alter that."

"Oh, well, when you put it that way..." I said, shaking my head and tossing a hand in the air in annoyance.

Harris leaned over to me and tugged on my elbow, pulling me back a bit. We allowed the women to out-pace us by a few steps and he leaned in close to my ear.

"See that mark on the back of Ekorius Emerson's neck?" he whispered, pointing to the back, right hand side of the taller woman's neck. I hadn't noticed it until now, but that's mostly because I wasn't looking for it. I squinted and tried to get a better look at it. Just above the collar of her golden dress bobbed a small mark. It looked like a tattoo of a cog. In the center of the cog, though, an immaculately detailed eye stared purposefully outward. The level of detail of such a small tattoo was genuinely impressive and almost unnerving.

I nodded to Harris, indicating I could see it and for him to continue his explanation.

"That's her graft. It's kind of a sigil of her Ward. She is from Ivoryfell. One of the reasons she was elected as their Council representative is because she is the prime example of what the citizens of Ivoryfell prize in society."

"Which is?" I probed.

"Logic and reason above all else. They prize intellectualism and are consummate perfectionists. If it isn't logical and you don't dedicate yourself to it entirely, then it isn't a pursuit worthy of your time."

"So what is she so good at?"

"It depends who you ask," Harris replied, "I've heard she is a masterful strategist. She is one of the prime directors of the union initiative for Emberwall, attempting to bring harmony to the various Wards. My guess is that she is that she's also very good at using that sword."

"I see," I replied. "So then her demeanor is simply the byproduct of her upbringing?"

"In part, yeah," Harris agreed. "But don't let that frosty exterior fool you. She is a profoundly caring lady and I've seen her do a lot of good for the city."

"You sound like you've spent a good deal of time with the Council," I added.

"Well, I am Dr. Fleming's apprentice, so I have to go with him when there are Proterezar meetings to ensure that his workload doesn't get too overwhelming and that he is able to focus solely on the matters of the Council. I occasionally listen in on their conversations and have the rare opportunity to chat with the various Council members when they're not busy in session."

"Well, hopefully she'll warm up to me at

some point -"

"What're you two whispering about back there?" Eva cut in.

Harris straightened and looked about as inconspicuous as a kid with his hand in the cookie jar. His big eyes looked off to the corners of the wall and I just shook my head.

"Politics," I equivocated.

"Oh?" she said, one eyebrow slowly raising into a questioning arch.

"Oh yeah. With all these Voidkin running about we were wondering who would be elected to Council." I offered matter of fact through an overtly cheesy grin.

"Riiiiight," she said, drawing out the vowels to indicate her tacit disbelief.

The Ekorius stopped abruptly and held up a hand. We drew up short and nearly walked into her. Everyone paused and waited as she turned her head to the hallway in front of us, the intricate Aug on her ear toward the dim corridor beyond.

"Sorry, I didn't mean anythin -"

She cut me off with a sharp look and a hiss. I stopped mid apology and everyone remained silent and still.

She kept her head tilted toward the hallway.

Her expression remained the same cool, composed nearly deadpan look she constantly had, but a moment later she slowly drew her sword from the sheath. I tensed at the sight of her sword but waited for instruction.

The Ekorius turned to the three of us, her eyebrows shot up and mouthed the word "Run!"

Well, crap.

CHAPTER TWENTY

We took off and followed the Ekorius's lead. She rushed down several more corridors and shut the thick metal doors behind us as we went. She didn't take the time to turn the heavy circular lock to fasten the door. Either whatever behind us was too close and we didn't have the time to lock them, or it was too big and would just bust through anyway.

I found myself taking a hard gulp as we ran, nerves kicking into gear. The three of them kept a brisk pace, but over the last few hours I'd gotten my footing back and felt like I could keep up. My legs were a good deal longer than both Harris and Eva and so I was having to work less to keep up with them. The Ekorius, on the other hand, was nearly as tall as I was and she was leading with bounding steps to set the pace. I noted that she ran with gracefulness yet poise. She didn't betray her calm and collected demeanor even in the pressure of a tense situation. Her muscles pulsed and revealed an athletic physique as they moved beneath her golden dress.

I couldn't help but wonder what we were running from, but part of me knew it was not a good idea to ask at this point. Ekorius Emerson came to keep us safe and I'm sure that's exactly what she was doing.

Fifteen minutes later and we were still running, taking the maze of the Network in stride. If I had been trying to keep track of where we were going, at this point it would've been hopeless. We had taken so many turns that there was no way I was going to ever make my way out without help. It's no wonder people get lost down here and never find their way free. Every hallway looked exactly the same, save for the occasional reinforced airlock-type door and metal box, apparently containing a landline.

To my left, Harris began to pant heavily, beads of sweat cresting his upper lip and forehead. His muscular build was useful in many circumstances, but he was not built to be a runner. Eva's face was set like flint and she was working to follow the taller woman. Being so short, though, Eva was having to work the hardest of all of us to keep up. There was dogged determinedness about her though and there was no way she was going to give up.

Another few minutes passed and finally the Ekorius slowed. We passed through another bulky door and shut it behind us. This time, we took the time to fasten the rotating lock and heard the thick metal hinges sink into place. We were all breathing heavily and I for one was not at all in shape for this kind of activity. My legs burned and I had a metallic taste in my mouth. Harris had his hands firmly gripping his thighs as he bent over, trying to slow his breathing. Eva stood with a hand on her hip, taking short breaths in her nose and blowing out her mouth.

"We have little time, but I must attempt checking in," Percipity said, walking to a phone box on the wall. She sheathed her sword and then repeated the same process as before to access the phone and held the earpiece to her ear. She waited a moment and then tried speaking to see if anyone could hear. Again, her face betrayed little information but she rapidly replaced the earpiece and the metal cover to the phone itself.

"Still no answer?" Eva asked, continuing to slow her breathing.

The Ekorius shook her head.

"How close are we to Thornsby's estate?" I asked.

"Just a few more passages and we should be to the Rigsturn district. Then we'll have to get up to the street and head to his home on foot. He never had a lift installed in his estate to the Network so it'll take a short while once we're on the street level."

I nodded and looked back at the locked door behind us.

"Do I even want to ask why we started running?"

"I'm uncertain as to what was trailing us, but it was something of the Void," Percipity said, tone cool and even as always. "It wasn't a Voidkin nor the Felmaven, that I can tell you. But it was making good progress on our heels and I didn't want to have a confrontation if we could avoid one."

"I second that," I said, raising my hand, index finger extended. "We should keep going then, if we're that close. I don't want to be trapped down here with another creepy demon thing if we can help it."

The Ekorius and Eva nodded and Harris took a deep breath, looking a little overwhelmed at the thought of running more.

"Come. This way." The older woman motioned for us to follow and took off at a pace somewhat tempered from before.

Another ten or so minutes passed before we turned down a long hallway with a lift at the end. We hustled over, opened the door, lifted the metal grate, and piled in the small elevator car, welcoming the opportunity to rest and breathe as the lift ascended.

It was a short ride to the surface and a quiet ping sounded as the doors opened. Again, we were greeted with the foreboding darkness of the Void once again. The nice thing about the tunnels was the fact that the darkness hadn't been able to get down there, for whatever the reason. It simply hung in the air anywhere outside of a building. Indoors, it seemed as though there wasn't as much issue keeping the darkness at bay. Out on the street though, it was so dark, it was difficult to see five feet in front of you.

The Ekorius took the lead once again and we fell into pace next to her. No one spoke as we hustled down the empty streets. The only sounds were the soft footfalls of our boots on the cobblestone ground beneath us. After a minute or two, my eyes adjusted again to the darkness and seeing was slightly easier.

We turned down the first street we came to and headed down the pathway. Percipity pulled her katana out and the rest of us followed suit. Harris and I drew out pistols and Eva slid the staff from her back and hefted it in one hand.

"We're almost there," the Ekorius leaned in close and whispered, "Two blocks down. Should see it on the left. Be ready for anything. Giles' message indicated some sort of ambush."

I nodded and felt the weight of the gun in my hand like a lead brick. I checked the safety and switched it to the off position, anticipating the worst.

"When we get there, Mr. Archer and Mr. Riley, you guard our flanks. Ensure that no one is going to get the drop on us from the sides or behind. Ms. Fleming will cover me and I will take point. In the event that we encounter anything, double check your target. In situations of low visibility and high stress, friendly fire is common. Don't forget that Ekori Horus, Yorke and Fleming are in there and hopefully Thornsby as well."

The three of us nodded and took positions to cover our respective target areas.

We rounded another corner and crossed the street. Buildings on either side of the street were dark and an unsettled feeling crept into my stomach. We pressed on and soon the line of buildings stopped fairly abruptly.

"There," Percipity said, pointing to a beautiful Victorian mansion at the edge of what I could see in the darkness.

It was the only building in the little bits of the city I'd seen so far that was not connected to any other buildings. Every other structure I'd passed by had shared both walls with the adjacent buildings. The Thornsby estate, however, was offset and even seemed to have a little bit of property. It was a three-story mansion with a gorgeous facade. It was a mixture of a throw back to Romanesque or Gothic brick style with imposing outer walls, but softened by intricate inlays of wood and metal, wrought together in beautiful gilded designs. Large turrets rose above the house and gave the entire compound a feeling of a small castle, while staying well within the boundaries of elegance. The grounds themselves were also beautiful. It was the first place I'd seen that had any semblance of acreage. In the front, a pony wall with an iron fence atop barred entry, giving way to a set of intricate metal gates at the center of the property. The gates were open and I could just make out a yard, nicely manicured and ready for a picnic.

The lights were off in the windows of the mansion, just as we had seen in all the other homes and businesses up to this point, but there was evidence that someone had already been here. We crept closer to the entry and stood at the edge of the property. There were no overt signs of a struggle or that anything had gone awry, but from the gate I could see the front doors were open slightly. Given the citywide state of emergency, there should have been no reason for anyone to leave the door open.

I checked my gun again, ensuring that the safety was indeed off and gripped it with both hands as we moved through the gate. A cobblestone path weaved its way to the steps in front of the door and we hurried to the house. I watched to the right as we rushed to the doorway, looking for any signs of life in the yard or coming from around the side of the house. I kept a wary eye out on the sky also, given that the Voidkin I'd met had been able to fly as well.

Ekorius Emerson nudged open the door with one hand, holding her katana in her other. I kept my eyes on the yard and watched behind us until Eva touched my arm and we moved inside.

The inside of the mansion was equally as impressive as the outside. Without the heavy settling of the black mist everywhere, it was easier to see inside. That said, it was still dark and eerie in the councilman's home. The foyer we stood in looked like a grand ballroom. The floors were a polished marble, much like those of the Proterezar chambers but that is where the similarities ended. Ekorius Thornsby apparently had a flare for the Romanesque and his decorating followed suit. Two huge Roman pillars bookended the doorway which opened into this ballroom. The ceiling soared up the entire three stories and drew your eye to the ornate staircase in the center of the room. The stairs from the upper levels parted halfway and looped down to the ground on either side of the room. In the center of the ballroom, a beautiful chandelier hung quietly, waiting to alight at the sound of laughter and fun.

There was a banquet spread out in the

middle of the room. Tables filled with all manner of delicious looking foods created a centerpiece to this hulking room. Industrial style bar tables dotted the room in a semicircular pattern, evidently placed so patrons of the event could enjoy their food and not simply have to hold it, but without giving way to the formality of a seating chart. It seemed as though Thornsby had planned on having a party this evening. Plates of half-eaten food and beverages periodically dotted the bar tables. By the looks of it, the Ekorius knew how to throw a cocktail party. Except for the fact that everyone was missing and there was some sort of nightmare going on throughout the world at this point. But, hey, when life gives you lemons, right?

Percipity and Eva moved as quietly as possible in front of us as they watched for signs of movement. The Ekorius went back to sticking those small devices on the walls we passed whenever she had opportunity. I still didn't know what they did, but maybe I'd have time to ask later. I scanned my sector for any signs of life or anything coming to kill me and was continuously relieved that nothing was there. That said, my nerves were constantly on edge given that everything very likely could change any second. I'd been working a desk job for years now and was *not* trained for this kind of action.

We moved to the center of the grand room, trying to figure out where Giles and the others might be. Several hallways and other alcoves presented options here on the ground floor. Off to the right, there was a pair of open doors that led into a huge kitchen. Pericipity looked around for a moment and then motioned to head upstairs. I gave a short nod and the four of us quietly made our way up the staircase.

I started to feel this nagging sense in the back of my mind as we moved through the ballroom and up the staircase. Something about this entire situation just didn't quite feel right. We ascended the stairs and the second story peeled off in either direction in a large hallway lined with doors.

"This may take a while," Ekorius Emerson said quietly.

We began checking each room as quietly as possible while being fastidious about our own safety. Harris and I stood in the hallway, guarding our backs while the ladies opened each door and did a quick survey of the rooms. Halfway down the hall, we switched and it was our turn to sweep the rooms. Every door we opened led to another lavishly decorated bedroom, guest room or some other kind of living space. One door I opened led into a bathroom that I could have lived in back home. The room itself was huge and had a massive tub, beautiful granite countertops, a large mirror and a walk in shower that could have fit fifteen people.

Every room we entered, the Ekorius placed one of her small tokens on the door and we progressed. On either end of the large hallway, the corridor shifted 90 degrees toward the back of the house and gave way to another stairway. This one was less ornate than the one in the grand room, but definitely still gorgeous and immaculate, like everything else in the house. Harris and I took up positions in the back of the group again and followed the Ekorius and Eva up the stairs. These stairs led directly to a single door made of thick dark wood.

Eva tried the knob but it was locked. The Ekorius placed her ear near to the door and listened for a moment. Satisfied, she stepped back and pulled a small device from her a compartment in her dress. With how tightly that dress hugged her, I didn't think there was room for anything in there, let alone a metal box that looked like a cigarette case. She opened the box and pulled out a long, slender piece of metal. It looked like a stir stick you'd get at a coffee shop, only this one was metal and could fold up into a small container. She inserted the skewer into the lock and closed her eyes for a moment. The metal glowed an odd shade of purple and then seemed to get sucked into the lock mechanism. A moment later, there was a soft click and the Ekorius opened the door.

I stared openly in amazement. Harris saw me, shrugged and nodded his head in the direction of the room ahead. It took me a second, but I quickly followed the others through the door.

The top floor of the mansion was one large room. It looked to be Thornsby's personal living quarters. There was a massive four poster canopy bed to one side with incredibly expensive looking sheets and a dozen or so pillows on top. A large chest sat at the foot of the bed and night stands bookended either side of the bed. In the center of the back wall, a huge fireplace sat dormant, but had evidently been used often judging by the level of soot covering the hearth. There was also a sitting area with several high backed armchairs and a chaise lounge was by a window, in case you wanted to enjoy the sun while reclining. This guy was living the high life, if ever I had seen it. Everything was crafted from the highest quality woods and furnishings possible. Yet, no one was around.

Percipity quickly moved through the room, checking the windows for any sign of entry. On the opposite end of the room along the same wall we entered from, there was another door leading out to the stairwell from the opposite side of the house.

"Nothing," she said, seemingly perplexed.

"There is still the main floor we need to check," I offered optimistically.

"True," she said again, still looking lost in thought.

Something about this entire situation was giving me goosebumps. It was clear from the call made earlier that something had happened here. As far as we know, it came from this house. Yet there was nothing here. Literally *no one* was around. Not Giles or August or Lydia or Thornsby or any guests who might have been banqueting downstairs.

We headed back down the stairs and swept the ground floor as well. It took about ten minutes of meticulous investigation, but still found no one. The entire estate was empty. We returned to the grand room.

"Did we miss something?" Eva asked.

"I don't believe so, but we can check again," Percipity replied.

That same nagging feeling crept up the back of my neck and my hair stood on end. As I stood surveying the scene, it dawned on me.

"Ekorius," I whispered as softly as I could manage while still getting her attention. Percipity glanced over her shoulder at me momentarily in a sign that she heard me. I continued.

"There are plates full of food and some half-eaten," I said, still scanning the hallways and back to the front door to make sure we weren't going to be attacked.

"I think he had some guests over tonight. But it looks like they've just up and left what they were doing. If they had been attacked, don't you think that everything would be a mess?"

She nodded and I continued the train of thought.

"So, if they weren't attacked, what happened to them? And in that case, what happened to the Ekori who came to retrieve Thornsby?"

"What're you saying, Finn?" Eva asked, stepping up to my side.

"Well, I don't like the idea of it, but what if the reason Thornsby didn't come to the Council meeting wasn't because he was in trouble. What if he *was* trouble?"

Eva and Harris glanced at each other as they processed the idea. A moment passed and their faces darkened. Everyone shifted stances and had their weapons at the ready.

It made sense. The ambush of the first retrieval team, the lack of any presence here at the estate. If he was in trouble, there would have been some sort of sign of a struggle. Thinking back on our first encounter with a Voidkin back at the Fleming's house, everything was a wreck. Granted, there had been a severe earthquake or something which had knocked over much of the decor, but when the Voidkin burst into the room, it left little unturned in its wake. We were barely able to make it out of there alive, let alone keep anything intact. The Thornsby estate, though, was completely untouched. It was even untouched by the earthquake. All of the paintings hung on the wall, all of the decorations and statement pieces were perfectly in place. *Nothing* was out of place.

Just then, the large front door slammed shut with an echoing boom. We turned to look but no one was there. Then, in rapid succession, the doors to the kitchen, hallways, alcoves and any other entryways slammed shut.

My heart began to race and my breathing intensified. I could hear much the same from Eva and Harris. Percipity seemed unfazed by the situation but her grip tightened on her blade. Then, the same darkness pervading outside in the streets of the city began seeping into the room. The already dark mansion gave way to an even more intense feeling of dread.

And that's when I felt the burning hot knife sear through my heart.

CHAPTER TWENTY-ONE

Have you ever been in *total* darkness before? I don't mean you've shut off the lights and gone to bed, though there is something to be said for that first moment of intense darkness. I mean complete blackness where you can't see your hand in front of your face and there is a world out there which you can't experience. If you get the chance, go caving once and turn off your headlamp. That's the closest I've ever been to complete and utter darkness. While you're in there and your eyes are trying desperately to adjust to the complete lack of sunlight, there are creatures *living* in that cave who are perfectly adept at getting around and living or even thriving in the darkness. It's unnerving to say the least. Our bodies weren't designed to function in that kind of environment, and yet there are creatures which treat the blackness of the depths like just another walk in the park.

The grand room in the mansion we were standing in had, in an instant, plunged into complete, unpermeated darkness. I cried out as white-hot pain ripped through my chest and clutched a hand over my heart. I fell to one knee and tried to breathe as the pain washed over me.

"Finn!" I heard Eva call out in the darkness. We were only steps from each other before the darkness settled in, but it felt like we were worlds apart right now. Sound reached my ears as if she was yelling through a long tunnel and it was everything I could to do to focus on breathing.

I flailed my free arm about trying to hit whatever had attacked me, but I swung helplessly through open air. After a moment, the pain subsided and my hearing returned to normal.

"Finn, what's going on?" Eva called out.

"Nothing, I just must have some residual pain from the surgery, that's all," I lied. I hadn't told anyone about my nightmare turned reality from earlier and this didn't seem like the time or place.

I tried to stand, but a new wave of pain

washed through my system so I decided to stay put. Getting up is too much effort anyway.

From the darkness beyond us, a gruff voice called out, "Eva! Eva! I'm here!"

It sounded like Giles, but there was no way to be sure where it was coming from.

"Dad! We're coming!" she called back and I heard her boots start across the polished marble. Percipity cut in from somewhere to my left.

"Do not move an inch," she said, her voice sharp and direct. Eva's footfalls ceased and I heard her begin to protest, but the Ekorius continued.

"Something is in here with us and it is not your father. Stay close and do not move until I say to."

I pushed myself to my feet and shuffled back toward Percipity's voice. I reached out and found the Ekorius's arm. A moment later, Eva and Harris bumped into me and we turned to stand with our backs in a square, shoulder to shoulder.

Just then, a rumbling laugh echoed on the tile of the room and bounced around us. It was hard to tell where the voice was coming from but it sounded louder than it should have.

"You are a resourceful bunch," a deep male voice called from somewhere in the darkness.

"Much more so than the buffoons who came here earlier."

There was a slight accent to his voice but it was hard for me to place. It sounded like a mixture between German and Jamaican but even saying that now, that sounds like a weird combination. It felt like he was shouting through a megaphone.

"Where's my dad?!" Eva called out.

"Hmm? Oh he's nearby, child. But at this point, speaking about him like he even exists is an unlikely probability." The voice broke out into laughter again.

"Which reminds me, it's time that you join him. I quite enjoyed watching you search my home as if I were simply going to be waiting here to be rescued. But I have bigger things to tend to and time grows short."

There was a clicking sound like a door unlocking and a rush of wind blew through the room.

"Oh, and Finn," the voice continued, "that little mark you've got? You're welcome."

"What?" Eva asked in the darkness, her face turned in my direction.

"I'll tell you later. We just need to get out of here."

"Blah, blah, blah." The voice chimed. The wind ceased and the darkness parted around us, carving a path before us to the kitchen door, standing open and visible while the rest of the room was still completely black.

"Don't move," Percipity said again, her cool voice hard and firm.

I held my gun tightly and remained still. Harris shifted on his feet but also didn't move. Eva chewed her lip and I saw her squeezing the staff in her hand trying to keep it together but I could tell she wanted to go find her father.

"Where is he!" she yelled back into the darkness.

"You'll find him in the cellar, along with the other fools who came with him." I could hear him smiling as he spoke.

"But you should hurry. He hasn't got much time," the man continued, "which is more than I can say for August and Lydia." His laughter started again and the four of us shifted uneasily.

"Galen, you're a coward and a fool," Percipity said. "Come here and face me and we'll be done with this charade."

"Oh pipe down you overgrown she devil," he snapped back. "The fun is just beginning and I get to be in the front row of the action. Think of me what you will, but history tells the story of the victor and I intend to make headlines."

Thornsby cleared his throat and continued. "Now, either you head down to the cellar and help your friends, or I open the front door and let the Voidkin do to you what they want. And believe me, it has not been easy keeping them from gobbling you down like a tasty dessert for the last few hours. Either way, I have an appointment with a very important client and I don't intend to keep him waiting."

Silence fell in the darkness and we stood there for a moment, unsure what to do next.

I saw Eva's muscles tense and she looked as though she was about to burst.

"We don't have time for this!" she said, starting toward the kitchen.

"No, Eva, wait!" Percipity called out, but it was too late. Eva dashed to the kitchen and the doors slammed behind her. The darkness lifted enough for us to see that there were dozens of pairs of writhing blue eyes at the windows outside the mansion. I felt a tremor rock through my entire body involuntarily and swallowed hard against the fear.

"Cogspit!" Harris muttered. Percipity turned to the kitchen door and snarled something I didn't understand and then took off at a run. Harris and I followed in step. The young man yanked on the doors to the kitchen but they refused to budge.

"Enough of this!" the Ekorius yelled as she lifted her katana into the air above her. The blade glowed momentarily purple and she cut a straight line down the crease of the door. The handle remained locked but the door swung wide. I glanced at the bolt as we headed into the room and saw it was melted in two, the lock still stuck in either door.

We hurried into the room but Eva was missing. There was a door leading outside on one side of the kitchen and a door that had been previously locked was now standing ajar. The Ekorius strode forward and headed straight for the door leading into the cellar. She threw open the door all the way and began descending the stairs.

The walls were close and there was a dampness in the air as we headed inside. The stone walls from the house above gave way to small bricks and the lights, unsurprisingly, would not turn on. We marched down the stairs, guns at the ready.

"Eva!" Percipity called out.

"Over here!" she cried out, frenzied.

We hurried the rest of the way down and saw Eva cradling her father in the corner of the cellar. Surrounded by barrels of wine and boxes, August, Lydia and Giles were crumpled in a pile like garbage to be thrown away, blood and dirt clinging to their bodies near large gashes and torn clothing.

Pericipity rushed to Eva's side and immediately grabbed the dark green medic bag from near Giles and began administering first aid. Harris and I went over to check on Lydia and August and found them alive, but only barely. Lydia had a large cut running the length of her face and the skin on either side had parted nearly to the bone, her thick clothes and leather holster shredded as if they were tissue paper. August was laying in a pool of tacky blood and his shirt was nearly ripped completely to shreds. His breathing was labored and shallow.

At once, Harris moved to August and ripped the remaining cloth from his chest. He began pulling it into strips and then handed me several strips as he moved to begin applying the makeshift bandages to the worst of the wounds.

I took the strips of cloth and tied them around Lydia's arm and leg to staunch the trickle of blood cascading down her skin and then tried wrapping one piece vertically around her head to cover the gash on her face. Percipity was working with the medic bag, getting out several different syringes and filling them with various liquids. A moment later, she injected a needle into Giles' arm and he gasped awake.

She took his face in her hands and stared at him, checking his eyes and looking at his reactions. Harris and I continued bandaging the other two as Eva held her father's hand.

It took only a moment, but after the injection Giles spoke hurriedly in a raspy, cracked voice.

"He's found Phantomsong. He's using it to draw in the Void. He's going to use it to find the other pieces of the Lightbane and eliminate the Arcmagus. There is still time but you must act now. He's still here. He needs his compound to finish the ritual. Don't let him win. Emberwall must be protected." His eyes rolled back in his head and he went limp once again. Ekorius Emerson gave no indication that anything he said was of note and continued administering injections to the others. Within moments, their breathing steadied but were still very much in critical condition.

"Bandage them tightly. One of us will need to stay here and make sure their vital signs are stable or they may bleed out while we deal with this mess. I will try getting ahold of Central once more before we chase after that monster."

"I'll stay," Eva said, looking down at her father with tears in her eyes.

"No, I'll stay," Harris said, tying off the bandage around August's torso. "I have the most medical training here and I should be able to fend off anyone who comes down here. Plus, you've been working on your skill much longer than I. If there is a firefight, they'll need you."

Eva nodded hesitantly, still cradling her father's limp form. She didn't resist Harris' offer and instead kissed her father on the forehead once and gently lowered him to the ground.

"Very well, we'll make haste," Percipity said, rising from one knee and picking up her katana.

"There must be a false facade or room in here somewhere, since we didn't find anything or anyone earlier when we searched the house," she said, looking intently at the walls and floorboards.

Not knowing any real first aid other than

bandages and gauze, I stood and started quickly inspecting the walls for signs of a concealed passage or a lever to open a door. They always have those in the movies, so why not here?

"Is there any chance we missed something upstairs?" Eva asked.

"There is always a chance, but the likelihood of us finding anything in the black Dreadmyre with Voidkin surrounding us is slim to none," Percipity answered, voice cool and collected as always.

Dreadmyre huh? How is it that I've been running around in the stuff for almost an entire day now and I just learned what it was called. Well, the more you know, I guess.

She continued, "Thornsby was speaking through a MAC projection system from a remote location earlier. It is likely he has the entire place equipped with surveillance and was watching us the entire time we were there. In each room, I placed an aural tension device which would've notified me if someone was sneaking up behind us from one of the rooms. I never picked up indication that he or anyone else entered the rooms we checked earlier, which means there is some other way to access his safehouse."

"Then let's get searching. Creepers like that

always hide something in the cellar," I said.

The Ekorius didn't reply but instead leaned her head against the wall and placed her empty hand against the cool bricks. She took a second to breathe and then small purple sparks bled out from her hand in a small shockwave across the wall.

I continued searching the cellar for any signs of escape other than the way we came in. Across the room, a shelf with various bottles covered in dust partially blocked a wooden staircase leading to a dual-paneled cellar door to what I assumed was the backside of the house outside. That was both a relief and unnerving, considering it gave the monsters more ways into our little confined party, but also provided a way of escape, should someone come from the inside door of the house.

I turned back to the group and saw Percipity still leaning against the wall, eyes closed and hand pressed firmly against the cold bricks. Eva was searching the floors near the collapsed party with little success and Harris was still busily tending to the injured.

"There is a door to the outside over here. It's closed and it doesn't look to have any way of securing it from this side. It might be of use if we need a quick out. Any luck with the walls?" I asked the Ekorius. She remained still and silent for a moment. Her look was one of intense concentration and I was not about to disturb a woman with a large sword from her work.

Instead, I started helping Eva search the floors and leaned in close to whisper.

"I thought that the whole Adrinyn thing was for mechanical stuff."

"It is."

"So how is she doing that on a solid brick wall?" I inquired.

"She isn't using Adrinyn. Ekorius Emerson is one of the few who is entrusted to use Lusynos without intense scrutinization of her every action."

"But isn't Lusynos what is empowering this whole mess in the first place?"

"Yes, and that's one of the dangers. One thing at a time though," Eva replied, eyes intently scanning the floorboards for any signs of a trap door.

A second later, the Ekorius's eyes snapped open and she stepped away from the wall. The purple sparks ceased at once and she sheathed her sword.

"There," she said, pointing to a section of the wall about fifteen feet away. She moved over to it and felt along the edges. There was an almost imperceptible seam along the brick which had been cut into the wall along the mortar line. Without whatever she had been doing, I doubt we would have found it.

Percipity felt the smooth bricks until her hand lingered on one longer than the others. Her hand tightened into a fist and she pounded against the brick once with surprising force. The brick sank into the wall an inch and the wall shifted and swung on a hinge, revealing a dark hallway beyond.

She drew her sword once again and gestured with her head that direction. I drew my gun, Eva picked up her staff and we walked to the newfound entrance. Before we marched onward, Percipity tossed one of the small disks she had been placing around the house to Harris. He caught it and turned it over in his hands.

"In case you run into trouble, press the center of the disk twice and it will alert me. We'll hurry back," she said as if she was reciting instructions from a manual.

He nodded his thanks and pocketed the device. He returned to his task and we headed down the hallway. Darkness stretched out in front of us and there was no telling what we were going to encounter.

I looked over at the two ladies as we started down the hallway. Ekorius Emerson looked calm and collected as always, katana resting comfortably in her hand at her side. Eva had a look of dogged determination, eyebrows furrowed and jaw set. Both of them seemed ready for a fight.

"So this is a total trap, right?" I said whimsically.

"Absolutely," Eva said.

CHAPTER TWENTY-TWO

We headed down the hallway at a brisk pace, the darkness deepening the further we went. After a minute or so, Eva tapped the bottom of her staff against the ground and blue-white light radiated from the small gemstone lodged in the tip. It helped, but only lit about fifteen feet in front of us. Granted, that was way more than if we had no light, but it wasn't much.

"So what are we getting into here? What was it your dad mentioned? Phantomsong?" I asked quietly.

"Somehow, Thornsby is invoking the Void here over Emberwall by using a relic of untold power created by an evil force during the Culling. The relic Dr. Fleming spoke of was considered an antiquated superstition. Phantomsong isn't even supposed to exist, let alone be here in the city. If Giles is correct and Galen *does* have Phantomsong, then he must be using it as a vessel for the Void," Percipity explained.

"So, as far as our involvement goes, we're looking to stop whatever ritual Thornsby has started and get the artifact? Got it. No big deal," I remarked playfully.

"In essence, yes. But I doubt that it'll be quite so direct," she replied.

I rolled my eyes, shrugged my shoulders and continued walking. Tough crowd.

"Any idea what the artifact looks like?" Eva asked.

"Up until a few moments ago I regarded it as a myth, so no, I have no idea what it could be," Percipity replied. "Remember, if we end up finding Thornsby he is likely not alone. August determined that there would need to be more than one person if this kind of ritual is going to succeed. Then again, Ekorius Horus didn't know that the culprit was going to be wielding a mythological relic." Her voice was calm and even the entire time.

I still could not get a good read on this woman. It was almost disturbing that she was presented with facts that directly contrasted what she had previously known to be *reality* and yet she was as cool as a cucumber. Considering literally everything in the last few days had been new and world shattering for *me*, the idea that there was some sort of powerful device being used to draw in evil powers from the corners of the planet to reign down terror on a strange mechanical world which included magic and cyber people was not too far beyond the potential of reality for me to accept any longer. Let's face it, I was probably going to need some severe therapy when this was all over anyway.

The hallway was barren, the brick walls cold and damp. We walked until the hall ended in an arched doorway. It didn't make sense to me why someone would build such a long and dreadfully boring hallway behind a fake wall in their cellar, but then again, I wasn't planning a major overthrow of society so who am I to say what crazy people do and don't do with their resources.

The door opened into a small room littered with crates, papers and all manner of things just haphazardly thrown about. Along one side was a wooden table with chains and harnesses affixed to it. In fact, it looked to me like a rendition of some sort of medieval torture device.

I allow myself to think too long about what the table might be used for and moved hurriedly to the other end of the room. There was a solid wooden door at the end of the room and light shining beneath it. Percipity held up a hand in a gesture of "stop" and she listened intently at the door. It didn't take supersonic hearing to notice that there was a low murmur of sound coming from the other side. It sounded like there were a number of voices all singing together, but they weren't a very good chorus. Scratch that, they sounded like they were chanting *somewhat* melodically and it sent a shiver down my spine.

I tightened my grip on the handle of my gun and readied to make an entrance. The Ekorius tested the doorknob and nodded that it was unlocked. She mouthed that she would count and then we would charge in.

"*One.*"

The hair on my neck started to stand up and I could feel my heartbeat pick up.

"*Two.*"

Sweat beaded my brow. Tension pulsed through my arms and legs and I felt like a coiled spring ready to engage.

"*Three!*"

As Percipity pulled open the door, something detonated to our right. A blast from behind sent me flying forward and I slammed into the wall. My head cracked into the bricks and then I blacked out.

CHAPTER TWENTY-THREE

I awoke. The first thing I noticed was the daggers hammering away at the side of my head. Every heartbeat blasted away a new throbbing sensation in my skull and everything hurt. It took a moment for the pain to lessen enough that I could even think straight, let alone open my eyes. That's when I saw that I was tied to a table, surrounded by hooded figures. My shirt was gone and there was a menacing black dagger suspended over my body.

"We would've done this sooner, Finn, but it is so much more effective if you're awake for the experience," an older man said, smiling down at me. He wore a dark crimson robe with the hood drawn back. He was probably in his mid to late fifties and sported a sophisticated crop of salt and pepper hair, cut close to his scalp in a military fashion and a nicely groomed beard. All in all, he was a handsome fellow, save for the scar dragged through his right eye.

"And now that you're awake, let's begin!" he said, pushing up the sleeves on his robes. A glance at his arm showed a tattoo similar to the one that was imbued above my heart, a cog with a skull in the center.

"Let him go Thornsby!" I heard Percipity call from somewhere off to my right. I turned and saw her and Eva both in chains, tied to a chair across the room from where I lay.

"Oh hush, you she-ape!" he snapped back. He eyed one of the hooded figures nearest to him and motioned towards where Emerson was bound. The hooded figure disappeared from view. A moment later Percipity spoke up.

"Don't you dare pu..." Her voice went muffled and the figure stuffed a gag in her mouth.

Thornsby centered himself and then looked down at me again.

"Now where were we. Ah yes, the ritual. *You*, my dear Finnegan," he said as he removed the dagger from the perch above my chest, "you are the main event."

"Or, and here's a thought. No." I shot back. Sarcasm isn't always the most refined discourse when in a stressful situation, but it certainly does make me feel better. I stole a glance at the rest of the room. It was a bland cellar room like all the rest, with the exception of this table and a creepy, legitimate cultist altar at the far end of the room. It stood several feet tall and sported the same symbol as our tattoos, only the skull was life size and I'm fairly confident it was a god-honest real human skull. The altar was covered in all manner of trinkets and splashed with different dark colors that I was hoping, realizing the situation I was in, was not dried blood.

Thornsby let out a small chuckle, reminiscent of the one heard earlier upstairs in the dark.

"Well, that would be interesting, for sure. But no, I've been working for days to get you here and now it's finally time to finish this. To be honest, it was easier getting you here than I expected. We're ahead of schedule!" His voice was an odd mixture of accents I couldn't quite place and though excited, carried a cold, sinister tone. An impish grin crossed his face and he gingerly felt the edge of the dagger to check its sharpness.

"Why me?" I asked, struggling against the hand holds on the bench. Turns out, I now know what the table out in the other room was going to be used for. Weird ritualistic cult people sacrifices where I would get to play the main role. Yippee for me.

"The question of the age, isn't it, Finn?" he replied, moving around the table from near my head to standing by my side.

"You see," he continued, his voice grizzled with age, "you have something no one else can replicate. And I need it."

"And what's that?" I pressed. Something to my right caught my attention and I flicked my eye toward it.

The older man just smiled down at me and patted the darkened spot on my chest. Burning white hot torment ripped through me and gave me a whole new understanding of the notion of pain. I stifled a cry and heaved against my restraints at the sensation. After a moment, the feeling subsided.

He ignored my question and turned to his companions.

"The ritual *cannot* be stopped," he said, his tone cold and businesslike, "Tau, Jabek, Gamma get to the package. Alpha, Laer, Sigma - Rendezvous at the shrine."

Six of the hooded figures turned and walked to a wall on the far end of the room. A moment later, the wall slid open as it had in the cellar and the men departed. Even with them gone, there were still a lot of creepy hooded figures filling the room.

Thornsby then motioned to his companions and the figures encircled the table. The chanting resumed and the older man lifted the black dagger high above his head. The chanting didn't sound like a language I was familiar with and the entire situation felt otherworldly. Wind started to rush into the small room and caught the robes of the cultists. The eye sockets in the skull on the altar along the back wall of the room light up with a blue-black intensity.

The chanting grew louder and I frantically tried to think of a way to escape. I pulled against the restraints but they were securely fastened to my wrists and ankles. My arms started to burn as I pulled harder against the shackle but they simply wouldn't budge.

Thornsby's voice rose above the others and the chanting grew to a frenzy. The wind continued to rush into the room, getting stronger each moment and was so loud it was nearly deafening at this point. Papers, dust and anything not nailed down swept through the air and the eyes on the skull at the altar burned bright. The dagger in Thornsby's hand began to glow a dark, fiery orange, and weirdly enough, occasionally pulsed with darkness. With each beat, all of the light in the room seemed to slowly drain into the dagger. Everything seemed dimmer and a muted darkness swept through the room. Even as this otherworldly symphony cast around me and the hooded figures drew in close, I saw Eva and Percipity wrestle against their restraints ineffectively.

This was it. This is where I die. I was saved and put back together like Humpty Dumpty by a nice man and his daughter just to be killed two days later by a crazy man with a black glowing dagger and his psychotic cultist friends. Great.

Finally, Thornsby called out in a loud voice "AND THUS WE ENTER THE ABYSS. THE DAY OF TIR'KALIS IS NIGH."

He brought the dagger down swiftly and plunged it toward my chest just above my heart. A deafening crack of thunder pierced the maelstrom in the room and suddenly everything went still.

CHAPTER TWENTY-FOUR

Time seemed to slow and stretch. The maelstrom of wind seemed to hover for a moment. The chanting cries of the cultists sounded distant and muted, the note they held, dragging on for an eternity. A crack of thunder echoed through the room. I braced for the worst and looked up.

An expression of confusion and pain spread on Thornsby's face. The dagger flew from his hands and instead, a gaping hole went straight through his wrist. A second crack of thunder crashed through the air and I felt one hand free from its restraint.

At once, everything sped back up again and a cacophony of yells and screams filled the air. I wasted no time. I reached over and unlatched the other brace holding my wrist to the table. I shoved Thornsby away and then quickly worked at the restraints on my legs. Thornsby stood stunned for a moment, but not long enough to let me get away. The older man grabbed me and started clawing at me. His right hand wasn't working, however, and the hole in his wrist spewed blood all over the table and, grossly enough, me. Soon, my chest and torso were covered in scratches and his blood.

"*No!*" he yelled in my face, mania touching his features. Again, I pushed him off of me as best I was able and flung off the restraints at my ankles. I jumped off the table and backed away from all of the robed figures. Harris stood in the doorway with his pistols, unleashing torrents of electric globes into the chaos, each shot punctuated with a crisp roar. Percipity and Eva were working to free themselves from their shackles and I turned to see one of the cultists throw a punch my direction.

I barely had enough time to register the swing and dip to the side, catching the blow in my shoulder instead of my jaw. I threw an arm up, blocking a second blow and immediately returned with a solid jab at the guy's stomach. I'm not a great fighter and I wasn't going for anything fancy. I just needed to buy time to get to the others.

Thankfully, enough years of playing soccer and having a bunch of guy friends who like to show their affection with 'playful jabs' has taught me that you have a nice block of nerves right above your stomach, below your ribs that sends shooting pain through your system and is what most people refer to as 'getting the wind knocked out of you.' My fist made purchase with his stomach and I was met with the satisfactory "oof" sound of the cultist not expecting the blow.

I pivoted and rushed past the guy as he cradled his stomach and got to Eva and Percipity just as they finished breaking free of their restraints. The general feeling of chaos and confusion delayed the other cultists from beating us to a pulp. Percipity flung herself from the chair and dashed to a small crate near the door, throwing off the lid. She reached inside and slid out her katana as well as a gun. In the same motion, she tossed the gun toward Eva and the young woman deftly caught it and in a second, had it leveled at the cultists with the safety turned off. Harris spewed an array of suppressive fire and managed to clip a few of the cultists. Thornsby cradled his arm, his expression wild and crazed.

"Kill them all!" he screamed. Without

preamble, an array of weapons slid from the concealment of their robes into the hands of the hooded figures and they charged toward us. The torrent of wind picked back up again. The sound overwhelmed the room and I saw Harris' bullets start arcing off target. Percipity tossed a gun to me and managed to snake out Eva's staff before one of the cultists was upon her. She turned and threw her arm in an upward arc, her katana in her right hand, catching the cultist full bore in his chest. Continuing the motion, she twisted and pulled her left hand up behind her and uppercut the guy with the butt-end of Eva's staff. The cultist screamed and was knocked backward a foot, landing hard on his back.

Finishing her turn, Percipity tossed the staff to Eva, who caught it as deftly as she had the gun before. To my side, Harris slowly made his way out of the arched doorway and over to us, still laying down a decent flurry of gunfire. They still had the numbers on us and I had lost track of Thornsby.

I checked the gun in my hand and raised it toward a frenzied cultist who thought of bringing a scythe to a gunfight. He managed to close the gap astoundingly fast and I barely had time to fire off a round before the curve of his blade met my skin. A burst of pain ripped across my arm and I felt the warmth of blood pool out in a gush. I hopped backward a step, sighted the maniac and pulled the trigger twice. Small ripples of piercing blue electricity shot through the man's stomach and continued into the floor beyond. Oddly enough, that didn't seem to phase him whatsoever. He charged at me again. I took another second to aim and pulled the trigger again. This time, the spark sailed through his forehead and his entire skull snapped backward with the force. A shower of blood and brain matter covered the room.

"I think this one is a bit overpowered!" I called out over the roar of combat to Eva.

"I don't think it's meant for people!" she yelled back, shooting her own pistol at a pair of frenzied cultists.

"I think it's more meant for the Voidkin!"

"Oh! Right!" I said.

Just then, a torrent of blue-white sparks and bullets soared through the air our direction. I grabbed Eva by the shoulder and yanked her behind the chair she had been tied to. Bullets sailed past and wood from the tables and chairs splintered into shrapnel around us. I hadn't seen any until this point and there was something weirdly comforting that the cultists had relatively normal-looking guns. Not everything was weird sci-fi laser blobs and nightmares. The feeling passed quickly, though, as a cultist sprayed the wall next to me with lead.

We hurried behind a table near the wall and with a heave, I forced it to its side. It wasn't a heavy duty table or anything and it wasn't going to stop a hail of bullets for long, but it was cover. If the crazy guys couldn't see us, it was harder to hit us. Blood dripped from my arm, but it wasn't a deep cut. The scythe earlier didn't manage to knick anything major.

I glanced over and saw Percipity holding her hand in front of her and bullets seemed to whiz by without hitting her. Occasionally, one would streak right at her and instead of harming her, a dome of purple light would materialize in front of her outstretched hand deflecting the projectile. She stood between the cultists and Harris, who was quickly reloading one of his pistols with another blue canister of super juice.

I nodded to Eva and the two of us both peeked out from around the table simultaneously. Immediately, bullets whirred past my head, only inches from my skull. I focused on a target and pulled the trigger. I had played enough video games that I should be good at killing cultists by now, but that just simply isn't the case in real life. When you're in the middle of a firefight, you aren't thinking about the loot the bad guy is going to drop or going for style points. In reality, I was freaking out and scared to death that one of these guys was actually good at their marksmanship and was going to send me back to Arizona in a body bag.

By now, the fight had devolved to where both sides were hiding behind what cover they could find in the cellar and repeatedly showering the others with bullets before needing to duck back into cover. Percipity was still holding a hand in front of her, but was now charging into the midst of the cultist forray. She caught the first guy unaware with blinding speed and strength and simply hewed him in half. Her katana crackled with a menacing purple electricity as she ran and bolts of lightning zipped out in front of her, stunning her opponents before she got there. By the time she made it through two of the cultists, Thornsby reappeared and was once again holding the dagger.

Phantomsong.

"Enough!" he said, raising the curved knife

over his head. The light in the room diminished drastically and the blade glowed eerily dark. He stood fifteen feet from Percipity and halfway across the room from the rest of us. The Ekorius was slicing her way through a mob of ten or so cultists who were trying frantically to bring their weapons to bear before she tore them to shreds, but it was evident that most of them were not going to make it.

Harris and I turned to Thornsby and started unloading our weapons at him. He, too, held out a hand and the bolts sailed past him with ease. He swung the dagger downward in front of him and a monstrous black wave sailed out from it and cut a path through the room to the fray where Percipity was fighting.

"Look out!" I yelled, but not quickly enough. The black force sliced straight through the cultist feebly trying to duel with Emerson and smashed into Percipity mid swing. She was lifted from her feet and thrown backward. Thankfully, the blow did not manage to sever *her* in half, but I was certain that another attack like that would not be good.

Percipity scrambled to her feet, blood trickling from her ear. I unloaded my pistol at

Thornsby and ducked back behind cover to reload my gun. I heard Eva's gun click with an empty cartridge and she ducked back behind the table as well.

"So, this is fun," I remarked sarcastically, sliding the lever and popping out the empty cartridge.

"I think you need to rethink your notion of entertainment," Eva replied, face set like flint.

"Any thoughts on what to do with Thornsby?"

"Give me a minute, I'll think of something." she said, her red hair whipping around in the wind.

I reached to my pocket to pull out another cartridge only to realize that they'd taken everything from me when we were knocked out earlier. I was tapped out and had nothing to help.

"Shoot! I'm all out of ammo!" I hissed.

"Me too," Eva said, tossing the gun aside. She hefted her staff with both hands. I peeked out around the table and saw Percipity backing up, putting a wall behind her for safety while cultists surrounded her. Her blade flashed purple for a second and then she moved with lightning speed arcing the blade in a halfmoon around her. Three cultists cried out in pain and fell back, holding their stomachs as blood pooled around their hands.

Harris's gun clicked next and I saw him reach for his last cartridge. He ducked behind a barrel near the door and reloaded the magazine into his pistol. There were still a few cultists left and Thornsby with the dagger.

"We gotta go!" Harris shouted to us.

"We have to stop him or the whole town is toast!" I called back. As we spoke, the room grew colder around us.

"We're running low on everything and that psycho has a literal relic of a Founder," Harris called back, pivoting out from cover and training his gun on Thornsby again.

Percipity finished off the last two cultists and the room fell unnaturally silent. Thornsby stood in the back of the room, holding the dagger outstretched in front of him. Percipity stood along the far wall, heaving probably twenty feet from him. Eva and I were still a decent distance away and Harris was even further.

Several cultists were moaning on the floor, but their cries were muffled by the sound of a man humming. Soon, the entire room was vibrating with the sound of it. It sounded like he was right next to my ear, quietly doing the dishes and humming a little ditty to himself. It took me a second to realize that it was Thornsby, his dagger was turning bright red with an unnatural black glow around it.

"Well played, Mr. Archer," Thornsby said. The humming continued however and it was seriously unnerving.

"You've ruined *everything*." He sneered in Harris' direction, but held the dagger very still. It continued to glow brighter, but with every passing moment, the room around us grew darker. It was as if the dagger itself was drawing in the light and heat. A frost was starting to settle in and I felt like I needed a jacket.

"You will not torment this city, Galen," Percipity called out, her voice cold as the room around us. "We were tasked with protecting and leading this city by the Ember. You've broken your oath and we will see to it that you are brought to justice under the articles of the Treswalen pact. Your friends lay dying and you're outnumbered. Drop your weapon and come peacefully."

"You seem to forget yourself, Ekorius Emerson," he replied, a smile touching the edge of his mouth. With the smallest flick of the blade in his hand, a tendril of black force rocketed across the room. Percipity raised her katana to intercept the blow, the purple glow still coursing through the blade. The force slammed into her, overpowering her will. Percipity let out a cry and her blade was thrown from her hand. The black washed over her body in an instant and she fell to the floor unmoving.

Thornsby turned his attention to Harris, his eyes shifting from the Ekorius to the young man. He started speaking but I ignored it and leaned in close to Eva, behind the shelter of our table.

"We have to stop him *now*," I whispered through clenched teeth.

"If you can distract him for a brief moment, I think I can get him. We're only going to have one shot at this, or I'm pretty sure we're all going to die," Eva said. Her tone was serious but there was a whimsy about what she said that seemed to be excited by the challenge. I nodded to her and popped up from my hiding spot.

Thornsby stopped mid sentence and turned his attention from Harris to me, one eyebrow raised.

"So quick for a death warrant, Finn?" he mocked.

"See, I'm sitting back here wondering how

you even knew who I was," I fussed with my gun in my hand behind the table.

"You're the reason I'm doing any of this, young man. Your arrival signaled an important shift in our world and I needed to capitalize on it," he said, bluntly.

The hole in the older man's arm had stopped bleeding for the most part, but he didn't look well. His features were gaunt and he was growing pale. I was certain that if he was going to incapacitate or kill us, it was going to have to be soon.

"To my knowledge, there are only a few people who know about my circumstances and you sure aren't one of them," I replied, trying to get some details while Eva got into position. From my side, she had shifted and was crouched with her free hand in a tripod holding her up on one side and the staff clutched in her other hand slowly glowing brighter and brighter.

"That is where you are mistaken, young man. You see, there are quite a few people who are aware of your arrival and are *very* excited to see you. In one way or another, you *are* the herald of Void and simply by falling into our laps, you've sealed the fate of this world."

I swallowed hard at that. My stomach

turned a moment and it took me a second to process what he said. I tried to play it off and at least keep my face neutral.

"Seems to me," I said, casually, "that you're the only jerk bringing the Void here and you seem to be failing to boot."

His face soured and he turned to face me dead on, Phantomsong pointed directly at me.

"You brandish, uncouth, rotten, impolite, back-water two bit nonchalant pretty boy! I will rip the life from your body so mercilessly that your very essence will wish that it had never been fabricated in the annals of history!" Thornsby took a deliberate step closer with every word.

I turned the gun in my hand over once and fidgeted with it as he spoke. I pressed two buttons on the handle of my pistol and waited.

"You know," he said, voice a degree cooler and more directly, "I can still complete the ritual with your corpse, it just won't have the same oomph like if I had finished it with you screaming out your last breath as I drove this dagger into your heart."

As he finished, I smirked and then pitched my empty gun his direction and unsurprisingly, he sidestepped it easily. Thornsby smiled and gave a small chuckle at my feeble attempt to stop him.

"Really?" he said incredulously. "Throwing your gun? Like that is going to - "

He was cut off mid sentence as the husk of my weapon exploded in a shower of metal and shrapnel. It wasn't a large explosion, given that my ammo canister was empty, but it was just enough. Thornsby was staggered momentarily and let out a muffled cry as bits of my gun showered his back with metal.

Seizing the opportunity, Harris let another salvo of electric bullets fly at Thornsby, two landing true - one in the arm and one in the side. Eva erupted from behind the table and closed the gap between her and Thornsby. About four feet from him, she stopped and leveled the end of her staff at him. The crystal in the end of the pole glowed bright, and suddenly Thornsby was lifted into the air, a soft blue aura affixed under his feet. Blue snakes of energy shot out from the end of her staff and coiled around Thornsby's arms, squeezing them together. He wrestled against the energy but was unable to break the bonds. Eva yanked on the staff and the blue tendrils moved with it, toppling Thornsby to the ground. Phantomsong, skidding from his hands and at once, the eerie humming that had filled the room abruptly stopped and the growing cold lifted.

I wasted no time. I dashed to the dagger and scooped it up, turning the blade to face Thornsby. More coils of energy blossomed out of Eva's staff and continued wrapping around the older man until he was bound, head to toe.

Thornsby's face was a mixture of anger and loathing. I know those sound the same, but there was definitely something in his features which led me to believe he wasn't *just* angry with us.

"I *will* kill you. All of you. The dark lord will rise and this land will reflect its true nature," he spat at us. Across the room, I heard Pericipity moan. *Good*, I thought, *at least shes alive.* Just then, Harris crossed the room and got in close with Thornsby and with one swift crack, hit him over the head with the butt of a gun. Thornsby went limp.

"Why!" Eva cried out.

"We have several injured Council members and no way of transporting him or them out of here without risking him using Lusynos on any of us. We don't even know what is waiting for us out there. There could be a hundred Voidkin waiting to tear us to shreds. Focusing on him would be a waste of resources that might help us defend ourselves."

"I had him bound," Eva said, her eyes and tone flat. She was clearly frustrated with his actions, but I have to say, I agree with him. He didn't kill the guy, just made sure he was a non-issue right now, considering our circumstances.

Eva turned from Harris and set her staff on the ground, pole end up so it stood perfectly straight into the air and clicked a button on the hilt. The tendrils of blue energy continued to emanate from the staff and bind Thornsby without her even holding the catalyst. She moved swiftly to Percipity and checked her vitals.

"She's still alive. Not in great shape, but she's alive," Eva said.

Harris moved to the Ekorius's side, evaluated her injuries with the quick, methodical training of a medical professional and then hustled out of the room.

From the hallway, I heard him call back "I'm grabbing the medic bag. Be back in two."

I took a moment to survey the room now that the chaos had subsided. Twenty or so hooded people littered the floor of the room, their blood staining the stone floors. None of them were moving or moaning any longer. The stench of death filled my nose and it was hard to keep from gagging. Thornsby limply hovered in place near where we had ambushed him and was being held captive by Eva's Adrinyn snake things. The altar in the corner with the creepy skull stood dormant, the eyes no longer glowing a bright blue. Percipity was on her back now and Eva was staring down at her with compassion, trying to make sure the woman didn't stop breathing while we waited for Harris. The dagger still in my hands was cold and heavy. I looked at it, turning it over in my hands. It was a long blade for a dagger and was a dark shining black. There was something written on it which I couldn't read, the symbols or language were unfamiliar to me and I couldn't make heads or tails of it. The bottom of the hilt had a small triangular shaped hole.

For now, I slid the weapon into my belt and walked over to Eva.

"We should find a way to call Central. Hopefully they can send help and we can get everyone out of here."

She nodded, not taking her eyes off of the Ekorius's quietly breathing form.

A few moments passed and we both

remained quiet until Harris returned, medic bag in hand. He moved quickly to Percipity and dug out a vial of something and began taking care of her. Eva and I moved to the side so as to be available to assist if needed but out of his way while he worked.

Eva turned to me and stared at me for a long moment, her crystal blue eyes digging deep. It made me a little uneasy, her stare. I couldn't tell if she was angry or upset or what it was she was thinking. Finally, she broke the silence.

"Finn, what do you think he meant when he said that your arrival sealed the fate of this world?"

"I'm trying not to think about it too much. Considering I don't know anything about this place, I can't imagine that my arrival did anything more than break my spine and make me miss home all the more."

She turned aside, watching Harris work as she spoke.

"Yeah, but you can't help but notice that things pretty much went to pieces after you got here. I know you've been here for a few weeks, but other than the last few days, you've been unconscious for it. And I can't help but notice the graft on your chest," she said, pointing to the small mark above my heart. The tattoo of a cog with a face in it.

"The graft?" I asked, thinking back to the conversation of the symbol on Pericpity's neck that Harris mentioned earlier.

"Yeah, the grafting is a term that we use here for the special sigil of your district in each Ward. There are dozens of different districts throughout Emberwall and getting your graft is seen as a right of passage for the youth when they turn 11. It is a symbol of pride for the bearer of their home. Each graft includes an element of their Ward and then the unique symbol of their home district. As you grow, it becomes a part of your identity. Often when a young couple is from mixed districts, they will find a unique way of showcasing their graft in a unifying manner." She paused and glanced at my chest again.

"Your graft there is a symbol. Except it's missing everything. The sigil of a Ward and a unique piece of a home district."

"So what does that mean?" I asked, looking down it myself. There was dried blood from Thornsby's wrist still caked on my skin but the black symbol above my heart was clear as day. From this angle, it looked more like a skull than a face, now that I had time to really study it.

"That symbol," she continued, "is the sign of Tir'Kalis." She nodded toward the altar in the back of the room.

"You mean I have a tattoo of a demon thing indelibly etched on my skin?!" I roared. I couldn't help but freak out a little bit. I'm not big on tattoos in the first place, although I have seen a few I thought were really interesting. Now, though, I'm marked by some sort of supernatural demon thing forever. Great.

"Yes," she said quietly, seemingly unsure of what to make of the situation. "How did you get the mark?"

I told her of the nightmare I had back at the Council quiet room and that I woke up in blinding pain and there was a mark on me.

"I don't really know what any of that means," she said honestly, "But we'll figure it out." She touched my arm gently. It was a small gesture and it was comforting to know that I had landed myself a friend in the midst of all of this mayhem. I still didn't really even know anything about this world or any of the people in it, but having a friend made it a bit easier.

I took in a deep breath and exhaled loudly. I nodded to her and then moved to the box where

Percipity had found our weapons from earlier. My ill-fitting shirt and jacket were tucked away in there and I took a moment to cover up. If I had been branded as a sympathizer with the crazies who started this whole nightmare, I didn't want to be walking around broadcasting that to the world.

"We should look for a landline and call in reinforcements," I said as I finished buttoning the last toggle on the jacket.

Eva agreed and we left Harris to tend to Percipity while we searched for a phone. Back in the cellar, Giles, August and Lydia were all sleeping, their wounds bandaged and covered with makeshift blankets Harris must have found in the basement. Thankfully, there was a landline on the wall nearby to the sleeping trio. It must have been the phone Giles had left the message with because the earpiece was covered in dried blood and there was a smudged black-red handprint on the side of the wooden box.

Eva stepped up to the phone and tried the to call the Council chamber. I leaned in close to try and hear through the earpiece. After one ring, a voice picked up on the other end.

"Yes?" A droning nasally voice said.

"Ekorius Blackwell, it's Eva Fleming," she

said. It took her a moment to outline the situation, but she pitched for medical attention and an escort to take Thornsby to a detention center.

"Very well. Several minutes ago the Dreadmyre lifted, the communication relays came back online and we've been dispatching teams to help secure the remainder of the city. It will be a long process but I have a few resources I can send your way," Blackwell replied. There was a sharp click and the line went silent.

Eva hung up the receiver and smiled.

"We did it!" she exclaimed. "The city is free from Dreadmyre and help is on the way." She leaned down and checked on her father who was breathing normally for a change.

We spent a few minutes tending to the Council members and I helped Harris get Percipity out from the secret room near to the others. The Ekorius looked awful. Her skin was growing pale and you could nearly see her veins through her skin.

"I'm worried about her," Harris said as we gently set her next to the other Council members. "She isn't responding to any of the medications I've given her and she isn't improving whatsoever."

"Well she did get hit with a blast of straight up darkness from a relic." I replied.

"True. I'm just concerned. She is stable for now, but hopefully the doctors will know better what to do and how to help."

I nodded and gave him a slight pat on his shoulder.

"I know you've done what you can. We didn't come here expecting any of this, there was no way to be prepared," I said.

A small placating smile touched his lips, but his eyes were still troubled. He glanced down at my arm and noticed the blood seeping through the white linen cloth of my shirt and nodded down at my arm.

"Think maybe we should bandage that?"

Honestly, with all the adrenaline and excitement, I had completely forgotten about it, which is surprising, given the fact that the cultist's blade had carved a nice curve up my entire forearm. It was still slowly bleeding, but it didn't hurt. That said, now that Harris drew my attention back to it, it began throbbing and stinging. Of course. It's amazing what your mind can compartmentalize while you're not focused on it.

"Nah, I thought I'd just slowly let myself

bleed out and really get the full effect of our little outing today," I said playfully.

He rolled his eyes at me, opened the medic bag at his waist and silently went to work dressing my wound.

Meanwhile, Eva went back to the chamber and retrieved the floating Thornsby. As she carried him into the cellar, it appeared he was no longer unconscious but seemed resigned to his fate by now. He had stopped struggling against the force binding him and remained quiet for the duration of our stay. He never stopped staring at me, though. His dark eyes remained fixed on me and every so often I glanced over and noticed him smirking to himself as he stared me down. Even beaten, that dude was freaking me out.

We sat there in silence for the most part, occasionally checking on the Ekori who were recuperating from their injuries. Giles seemed to have been the least wounded of the original team. His arms were bandaged thanks to Harris and there was a large gauze pad across part of his face. Blood had begun to seep into the gauze, but it didn't seem too drastic. His clothes were tattered and bruises poked through wherever skin was visible.

Lydia and August didn't seem to be quite so lucky. I don't know if there was an explosion or if they were simply ambushed by all those cultists from earlier, but they looked pretty dire. Both of them were breathing, but it was shallow and labored. Lydia's brown curly hair was partially disintegrated and she was missing an eyebrow. Her face was completely swollen to the point where one eye was forced shut by the skin. Her garments had been mostly destroyed and her skin down the left side of her body was either puffy white blisters or missing altogether. Harris had done what he could to bandage her, but there wasn't enough in the medkit to cover her.

August was the worst of the lot. He was also burned and bruised all over. I gathered from the state of his face and torso that he had probably been in front when they were ambushed. His entire front was mangled and blisters, cuts and large sections of missing skin marred the once spry, excited young man. On his right arm, a small tattoo was visible, a cog surrounding a woven cord superimposed on a burst of stars.

Thankfully, everyone was at least alive.

The silence was a nice reprieve from the hellscape we just endured, though it left me alone with my thoughts and Galen Thornsby had just dropped a bombshell in my lap. I was more confused than ever, and the man sitting bound before me seemed to have answers. I wanted to pepper him with questions, but I doubted he would just willingly open up and tell me everything I needed to know. Instead, I let it be and tried to help Harris to the best of my ability, which is admittedly poor.

It took an hour or so for help to arrive. Maybe it was shorter than that, but sitting in the cellar with Thornsby staring at me, rarely blinking, made time seem to drag on. Finally, several armed guards like the ones I had seen in the Council chamber rushed into the cellar, guns drawn, working as a unit. Upon seeing us they signaled the 'all clear' and immediately went to work on the wounded. They pulled small spheres from their pockets much like the one Harris told me about when they saved my life from falling through the sky. One of the officers held the sphere above Giles and activated it. The air around Giles distorted and he began levitating off the ground. The officer then held the sphere and was able to easily lift Giles out without hefting him over his shoulder and it seemed as though Giles was weightless, like being in water. A few other officers did the same for August, Lydia and Percipity and they brought the injured Ekori out of the room.

Two other officers, clad in more than the standard basic uniform, with thick plated armor and helmets marched down the stairs with a vaguely casket-shaped metal canister between them. They marched over to Thornsby and lifted him, still bound by Eva's Adrynin staff and placed him inside the canister. Eva switched off the button on the staff and deactivated the forces binding him. The officers then shut the lid and fastened the lock on the side. There was a viewing window for the containee to see out to the world and Thornsby laid there, staring blankly ahead. Everything about him gave me shivers. I was grateful when the officers hauled him up the stairs and out of sight.

"What was that?" I asked, leaning over to Harris.

"Those were members of the Hand. They're the elite police force of the city and are specially trained to deal with rogue Lusynos users. I'm not entirely sure what they put him in, but I've heard they've created special devices to help mute the abilities of those apt in Lusynos if ever their powers get out of control. Or, I guess in this case, if they get out of control."

"I'd say a little of both on this one."

He smirked and elbowed me in the side.

Eva took a moment to quietly discuss the situation in the secret chamber down the hall with the lead officer and suggested perhaps backup might be necessary for clean up.

"I'm sorry ma'am, that will have to wait," he replied, his tone clipped and official. "There are a significant number of areas throughout the city which are in need of large-scale decontamination and this situation is curbed for the time being. I will add the location to the list and we will get to it as time allots."

She nodded and bid him her thanks and then walked over to me and Harris.

"Well, what now?" She said.

"Food," Harris said, a hand on his stomach. She smiled at him and nodded.

We gathered our things and made our way up the cellar stairs back to the kitchen. I stopped a moment as we reached the top of the stairs and the other two turned back to look at me.

"I…" My voice trailed off. I'm not sure what to say. It's been a crazy two days since the first rumbling happened and I pulled myself off the bed. I hadn't even seen the city that I was trapped in and now, for them, everything was going to go back to normal. But nothing here was normal for me. I was a stranger, trapped in a strange place where magic and controlling machines with your mind were a normal part of everyday life and was just told that I was the harbinger of doom. I have no idea how I got here and that leaves me few options for finding out how to make it home.

The look on my face must have said something because both Eva and Harris walked back down the steps and stood next to me. Eva put a hand around my shoulders and squeezed gently.

"We'll figure it out together," she said.

"Yeah. We'll be here to help you and we'll find a way to get you home, okay?" Harris chimed in.

I smiled and felt my face flush. I knew the future was going to be a rough stretch, but having people to rely on was going to make it easier. I nodded my thanks and we continued up the stairs. Back in the kitchen, light flooded into the room now and it seemed like mid-morning. The light was bright and fresh, though not direct.

We walked back through the kitchen and into the great room where the banquet was set. We walked to the front entry and Harris pulled open the big wooden doors. Light swept through the opening and it took a second for my eyes to adjust. As he opened the door, I was greeted with a view like none I had ever seen before.

Beautiful Victorian buildings lined tight cobblestoned streets. It looked like everything I had imagined England was like back in the 1800s, but there was a beautiful modernization of it with metalwork and intricate designs which gave it an industrial chic look about it. The beauty of the buildings was accentuated by the sheer height. My eye was drawn up and up and up as the buildings continued to shoot off into the skies at an alarming height. Each level was crossed with metal walkways and I could see people milling about on an area another level up, seemingly readjusting to life after the darkness. The sky above was crystal blue and the sunlight cascaded across the city.

Amidst the splendor, there was lingering evidence of the horror from the last few days. Small fires burned sporadically among the various walkways, rubble piled in the streets and anyone outside seemed huddled and walked quickly, glancing about frantically as they walked.

Eva took a deep breath and looked up and down the street, seeing people cautiously returning to their normal lives after days of such an ordeal. We stood there a moment, Thornsby's den of nightmares behind us, the city before us. Finally, Eva smiled and looked over at me.

"Finn?"

"Yes?" I said, mouth agape and eyes still glued to the sheer size and beauty of the city.

I heard her light up and an excitement edged into her voice. She and Harris put a hand on me as she spoke.

"Welcome to Emberwall."

www.ingramcontent.com/pod-product-compliance
Lightning Source LLC
Chambersburg PA
CBHW030554180626
46816CB00005B/1542